Sounds Like a Cheerful Train Today

By

Kenneth Lee McGee

For Denise

Who years ago gave me
credit for having the courage,
if not the skill,
to tackle a rather
controversial subject.

I would like to thank everyone
who has taken time to visit my website
or my Amazon author page.
I appreciate the support
and kind words.

Thank you Cory Woodward
for the cover photo.

Prologue

"Tucker, I realize your parents just left, but you should call them back," Dr. Galuten said. "I don't think it will be much longer."

"I will call them," Caralyn Dawson volunteered.

Tucker McKay clenched his jaw and nodded. He returned to his chair at his wife's bedside and took her hand.

Nancy Young McKay's parents sat against the wall and alternated staring out the window and checking the machine monitoring their daughter.

"Mom, I'm sorry, but Dr. Galuten thinks you should come back," Caralyn said.

Sarah McKay took a deep breath, looked at her husband, Jim, and said, "We will be there as soon as possible."

Caralyn ended the call and walked over to Mr. and Mrs. Young. "You should tell her something. She might be able to hear you."

"Thank you, Cara," Mrs. Young patted her hand and moved to the empty chair on the opposite side of Nancy's bed from Tucker.

Andrew Young wiped his eyes, stood behind his wife, put his hands on her shoulders and whispered. "Go ahead, Donna. I don't know what to say."

Caralyn walked around the bed, put her hands on Tucker's shoulders and squeezed. She looked at the clock and noted the time. 8:01.

Mrs. Young whispered to Nancy for another minute, then she and Mr. Young moved back to their chairs against the wall. He put his arm around her shoulders and moved her head to his chest.

"Cara, you should sit down," Tucker said.

She walked around the bed, sat down and took Nancy's other hand and allowed the tears to flow. She watched as the nurse entered, looked at the monitor and turned off the alarms. The nurse moved to the doorway, stood beside Dr. Galuten and whispered, "She's gone. Do you want to check and call it?"

He nodded and walked up to Tucker. "I have to make sure."

Tucker clenched his jaw and nodded once, ever so slightly.

Dr. Galuten checked Nancy for a pulse and turned to Tucker, put a hand on his shoulder and said, "It's over. I am sorry for your loss."

Caralyn let go of Nancy's hand, looked at the clock, noted the time, 8:07, and sobbed.

Tucker squeezed Nancy's hand and lowered his head to the edge of the bed.

Dr. Galuten and the nurse left the room. No one else moved until the McKays rushed in.

"We're too late," Jim whispered after seeing Tucker and Caralyn.

"She's gone, Mom," Caralyn rushed into her mother's arms.

Dad moved behind Tucker and rubbed his shoulder. "I wish I knew what to say, son."

Tucker lifted his head, looked at Nancy, then patted his father's hand. "Just because we knew it was close, doesn't make it any easier."

"I'm sorry we didn't make it back in time," Sarah said to the Youngs.

"You've been with her all night for the last week," Mrs. Young said. "We couldn't ask for more."

"Would you like more coffee, Donna?" Sarah asked the next morning.

"I shouldn't, but half a cup, please."

Sarah poured the coffee then sat beside Mrs. Young. "I wasn't hungry, but Caralyn made me eat. I could make something for you and Andrew. Tucker hasn't eaten a thing since yesterday morning."

Mrs. Young looked over her shoulder to where Tucker, his father and father-in-law sat with blank expressions. "He needs to eat to keep up his strength."

"I'm not hungry," Tucker said.

"You have to eat. I will make pancakes and scramble some eggs." Sarah got up and walked around the counter to the fridge. "He has bacon. I'll make that too."

"Andrew! You need to make Tucker eat something," Donna said. "All of you need to eat. We can't sit around moping. We have to make arrangements for her service."

"Okay! You need to shower and get dressed, Caralyn Ann," Beth Dawson said. "I know you are hurting, but you have to be strong for Tucker." Beth walked to where Caralyn lay on the couch, grabbed her hands and pulled her to a sitting position. "You need to be upstairs with Tucker and the McKays."

Caralyn looked at the ceiling. Her apartment was directly beneath Tucker and Nancy's unit.

"Ray is coming over. He will be here in thirty minutes. Do you want him to see you like this?"

Caralyn stood up. "Fine! I will get dressed. Are you guys coming to the funeral?"

"Yes, but you need to help Tucker and her parents with the details."

"We made the calls to family yesterday. The people from the funeral home were coming to pick her up today, I think."

"Is there anyplace large enough in Stockton Woods to hold the service?" Beth asked. "The church isn't by any means."

"I think the high school gym would be the biggest place in town unless we have the service outside."

"That's not happening." Beth waved her hands.

"Tucker and her parents will have to decide."

Caralyn showered and dressed. Ray Gardner, Beth's longtime partner, sat on the living room couch. He stood up when Caralyn entered.

"Thanks for coming over," Caralyn said.

Ray hugged her and whispered, "I'm sorry about Nancy. You were close friends and it can't be easy to deal with her loss."

"It won't get any easier after the funeral."

Chapter One

Caralyn, you don't have to stand by me the whole six hours." Tucker stood beside the casket in the Livingston Funeral Home. "I'll be okay if you want to visit with friends."

"You stayed with me for Grandma Florence's wake. I'm here to support you. Just don't introduce me to her family as the delinquent again."

Tucker grinned for a split-second. "I only introduced you like that to one of Nancy's aunts and uncles. You've met them before. George and Bessie. They used to live past the grade school when we were kids. He got Mr. Young a job with the county. That's why they moved to Stockton Woods."

"One of her great aunts thought I was Nancy's little sister."

"I've heard people say you are her cousin and others think you're Lloyd's baby sister."

"Get out!" she poked his side. "Do I still look like a kid to you?"

"No, but you behave like one at times."

"Where did Nancy live before?" Caralyn asked while shaking hands with another local well-wisher. "She might have told me a long time ago, but I can't remember."

"They lived on a farm outside of Vernon Heights. I can take you past it sometime, but the old farmhouse was demolished several years ago. A doctor from Idaho bought the land and built a new house."

Several more couples spoke to Tucker.

"Who was that?" Caralyn asked. "They looked familiar, but I don't know their name."

"The Balances. They were neighbors of the Youngs until we graduated from high school. They had a son in your class, but he was killed overseas."

Caralyn watched the Balances walk away. "I remember him. He was always upbeat and never made fun of anyone."

"He was a member of the church. He talked about becoming a preacher for a while."

9

"He probably should have. He wouldn't have joined the army," Caralyn whispered.

Sandy walked over carrying the baby. "Tucker, I need to take a break. Lee Andrew is getting restless."

"Go ahead, Sandy. We will stay with your parents."

Caralyn peeked at the baby. "He's adorable."

"Thanks, Caralyn. He's been a handful at times."

Later, Tucker introduced Caralyn to several of his Chicago Bulls teammates, who had made the trip to pay their respects.

"They are so tall, Tuck. They make you look like a normal-sized guy. Kinda puny in a way," she whispered.

"Alphonse is seven feet tall, so I am short compared to him."

"I hope he doesn't get upset because everyone will ask about the weather up there."

"He's used to it." Tucker pointed to a lady in a wheelchair being pushed by an elderly man. "That's Grandma Chapman. Mrs. Young's mother and her father. They live in Ohio."

"She used to talk about them, but I don't remember ever meeting them."

"They didn't make it to the wedding because of her health."

An hour later Caralyn whispered, "There are more members of the Young and Chapman families than all the people who live in Stockton Woods."

"Not quite, but there are a lot of cousins and many of them live in the area," Tucker said.

"There's Grandma and Grandpa," Caralyn said.

"I told them they didn't have to come," Tucker said.

Caralyn nudged his side. "Did you think they would stay home. You're their favorite grandson."

"Not so, but you're their favorite grandchild."

"And I'm not even related technically."

"Try telling that to Grandpa."

"Shush," Caralyn said.

10

Mom McKay walked up to Caralyn later. "You should get something to eat before you pass out."

"I'm okay, Mom. I ate a couple cookies about an hour ago."

"It's almost seven. You should eat something while the line's not as long. Richard, Derren and Davey are back there. You should talk to them."

"Will you be okay if I take a break, Tuck?"

"Go ahead, but I saw Beth and Ray walk in a minute ago. I didn't know they were coming."

"I wasn't sure they would make it either," Caralyn said.

She excused herself and found the room with the refreshments.

"How's Tucker holding up?" Derren Stanfield asked. "I told him Natalie would be here tomorrow. She couldn't get off work both days."

"That's okay." She looked up at Richard and said, "Well, Mr. Laderman, How's it feel to be a hotshot New York attorney?"

He shrugged and said, "Don't have a clue. I'm not a member of the bar yet. Plus, I've been working a hundred hours a week, and that's in the slow times."

"I'll grab you something to drink and one of those fancy, little sandwiches, Cara," Davey Stanfield whispered.

"Thanks. I was about to pass out, but I wasn't going to leave Tucker on his own."

Davey brought the snacks to her and stood behind her with his hands on her shoulders as she ate and talked to the guys.

"Derren, are you staying with your folks tonight, or driving back to West Memphis?" Caralyn asked.

"Natalie said I should come home."

She turned to Richard and asked, "Where are you staying?"

"In a suite at the Butler Hilton."

"You're a goof. There are no suites at any motel in Butler."

"As I learned earlier."

"I need to talk to Grandma and Grandpa," Derren said.

"I'll go with you," Richard said. "I didn't realize Nancy's family knew everyone in Southern Illinois."

11

Davey squeezed Caralyn's shoulders and asked, "Are you going to make it through the next couple days?"

She leaned into him. "I will for Tucker's sake. Can we sit down? Where's Melissa?"

"Taking care of her sister's baby. She might stop in later, but we will be here tomorrow."

Caralyn removed her shoes and rubbed her feet. "I hate wearing pantyhose and these shoes are killing me."

"Would you like a foot massage?"

"Yes, Davey. That would be awesome."

He grinned and said, "Tell Melissa. One of her friends does that for a living. Personally, I'd never touch your smelly feet."

She wrinkled her nose at him. "I would smack you, but it's not the proper place. Remind me to smack you some other time."

"Did you have a black dress, or did you buy it this week?"

"I bought it two days ago. Do you think it's too short?"

He looked and shook his head. "It looks nice."

"I'm worried about Tucker."

"That's expected."

She took his hand and said, "No, he's in denial now. Or whatever. He's been too distracted to take care of stuff at the apartment. He's lost without Nancy. I was up there the other day, and he hadn't cleaned up the kitchen or done any laundry. I had to force him to shower and shave. He looked like a bum."

"You and Nancy were like sisters. I'm concerned about you, little cousin."

She squeezed his hand. "You're sweet, but I'll be okay."

"Yeah, you can say that, but I know you better, Caralyn. You will put on a face like everything's okay and not let anyone see under the mask."

"I have to be strong for Tucker." She rubbed her feet again then put on her shoes.

They stood up and Davey hugged her. He kissed the top of her head and whispered, "You know where to find me. I may not be the sharpest arrow in the quiver, but I'm the best listener in the Woods."

12

She grinned and said, "Where did you hear the word quiver?"

"In a Robin Hood movie most likely," he answered putting his arm around her shoulders. "Come on. Let's talk to Grandma and Grandpa before they leave."

Beth saw Caralyn talking to the Stanfields.

Ray glanced at the people still waiting in line. "Was Nancy, or her family, big shots or something?"

"Not that I know of, but she was married to Tucker. He's probably the most famous person to come from Stockton Woods."

"Didn't Abraham Lincoln sleep in a hotel in town before he became the president?"

Beth laughed and answered, "That was George Washington who slept in every little town in Virginia. No one famous has ever been to Stockton Woods unless you count the time the train broke down with Babe Ruth on board. He got off and played catch with some of the kids."

Ray ran a hand through his ponytail. "Are you serious, or what?"

Beth shrugged. "That's the legend. It was printed in the paper so it has to be true. The *Stockton Woods Express* wouldn't print it otherwise."

"Beth! I wasn't sure you were coming," Caralyn said. She hugged her sister and smiled at Ray. "Thanks for being here."

"It appears we aren't the only people who drove down from the city." Ray pointed to another tall man. "He plays for the Bulls."

"I'm glad you bought a new dress, Cara. The one you had at home didn't look as good."

"Do you think anyone will notice if I wear it tomorrow?"

Beth shook her head. "No one will care. How's Tucker doing? And don't give me that crap about he's holding up considering the circumstances."

"I'm worried about him."

"Should we be concerned? More than normal, I mean."

Caralyn shook her head. "We will take care of him."

13

"Do you know many of her family members?" Beth asked.

"Not all, but I met some at the wedding." She looked at Mr. and Mrs. Young. "They have to be devastated, but they have this faith in God that seems to give them strength."

"We're staying in Butler tonight."

"You could stay at the house with me," Caralyn said.

"Which house?" Beth asked.

"Grandma's house. I stay there now when I come home. When Tuck and Nancy would come home, they would stay with her parents."

"Thanks, but we already made the reservation," Ray said.

"We will be here for the funeral, but we will head home after it's over."

"I understand. I imagine Tuck and I will be here all week. Oh, could you check my place? You have a key to get in, and I'll give you my key for the mailbox."

"Sure. We can stop by the apartment when we get back. Give me a hug, and we'll see you in the morning."

At nine there were still people in line. Caralyn stood beside Tucker until the last person paid their respects.

"I didn't think there were this many people in the state," Tucker said. He turned to look at Nancy. "I hate to say it, but she doesn't look like I remember."

"No one ever does, Bubby." She held his hand until he turned away from Nancy.

"Do you need a ride?" he asked.

She shook her head. "Davey's waiting. I told him we could order a pizza or something. He made me promise I would eat something tonight since I haven't eaten much all week."

"I didn't see Melissa. Did she make it?"

"Briefly. Davey said she will be here tomorrow."

Tucker squeezed her hand and moved a curl behind her ear. "Don't stay up too late, okay?"

"I won't. You can call me if you need to talk, or need help getting to sleep."

14

"I will be fine."

Caralyn met Davey in the foyer.

"Are you ready?" he asked. "Your parents left a few minutes ago."

"I'm ready. Everyone's gone except for Tucker, Nancy's parents and Sandy. This has been one of the longest days of my life, Davey. I need something to eat faster than a pizza."

"We could swing by The Curve. It will still be open."

"Good."

They ordered burgers and fries and he drove her home.

"There should be pop in the fridge. I'm going to change. Don't eat all my fries," she ordered.

"I'll save you a few."

They sat at the kitchen table to eat.

"I probably shouldn't have had a Coke," Caralyn said. "The caffeine will keep me up."

"We can watch a boring movie. That might put you to sleep."

"At least I'm in my pajamas if I do fall asleep."

She found an old movie on channel twelve and they sat on the couch to watch it.

"I'm letting you know up front if you fall asleep, I'm not carrying you to bed like Tucker used to. You're too heavy now. I don't need a broken back."

She slugged him with a throw pillow. "I don't weigh as much as Melissa, you twerp."

"Cara, are you awake?" Davey asked two hours later. When she didn't answer he stood up and shook his head. "I should leave you here, but I'll be nice." He retrieved a pillow and blanket from her bedroom. "You owe me for being extra nice to you this week." He moved her onto her back and covered her. "See you in the morning, Caralyn." He turned off the lights, locked the house and drove home.

Chapter Two

Caralyn walked across the yard to the McKay house and entered the utility room.

Tucker saw her first and asked, "Are you riding with us?"

"What time are you supposed to be there?"

"Nine thirty."

"At the gym, or the funeral home?" she asked.

"The funeral home."

"Will the casket be open?"

"It will be the last time for family to see her," Tucker said rubbing the back of his neck.

"You are her husband. You can choose how you want it."

He waved and said, "I know, but Mrs. Young asked for it to be open at the funeral home. I would feel selfish if I went against her wishes. She was my wife, but she was her mother her whole life. Do you get my meaning?"

"I understand. Are Mom and Dad ready?"

"We will be ready in five minutes," Dad said. "Sarah wants to know if you ate breakfast?"

"I ate a banana. Part of one," Caralyn answered. "Do you have any idea how many people will fit into the gym?"

"They have crammed a thousand in there for concerts. Do you remember when Fridays At Five played a benefit in 2000?"

"I remember. I was eleven and Tucker took me to the show. We were close enough to the stage to see them sweating."

"They would never play a small town now. They're too famous," Tucker said.

They arrived at the Livingston Funeral Home and parked across the street.

"That's Mr. Young's car," Tucker said. "I hope they haven't been here too long."

"We are early," Dad said.

They went inside and Caralyn picked up one of the memorial cards. She read the Bible verse and asked Tucker, "Did you pick this out?"

16

"Her mother suggested it."

"Psalm 23 is used for funerals quite often," Dad said. He looked at Nancy's photo and the date. June 11, 2010.

The Stockton Woods High School gym was the only place in town spacious enough to accommodate the large number of expected mourners. By the time the family arrived, every chair not reserved and every spot in the bleachers was filled.

"Do you want to sit with me?" Tucker asked Caralyn. "I'm supposed to sit with her parents."

"I'll stay with Mom and Dad, Tuck. There might not be enough room for her family."

"The reserved seats are for my family, too, Cara."

"I know, but I'll sit with Mom."

"Okay, but I want you next to me at the cemetery."

She nodded and followed her parents. They sat in the same row as Uncle Carlton and Aunt Mary.

"Are you hungry, Cara?" Davey asked as she sat in front of him.

"Yes, but I can't eat because my stomach's full of crazy butterflies."

"I've got some crackers if you need them later."

"Thanks, Davey. Hi, Melissa," she said and then saw Derren, Natalie and Richard two rows back. She waved and sat down.

When the people from the funeral home brought in the casket, she saw Tucker's shoulders shudder. *Oh, Bubby, I should have sat next to you. I'm so sorry. Will you ever forgive me?*

After the service, the funeral procession slowly wound its way through town as it snaked to the Lincoln Ridge cemetery. The wind blew gently through the large maple trees surrounding three sides of the old cemetery as everyone exited their cars. They walked along the gravel road and made their way to the tent erected over the freshly dug gravesite. The funeral home staff worked feverishly to place as many of the floral arrangements inside the tent as possible. Mr. and Mrs. Young, Sandy and Lloyd sat with Tucker in the front row along with the McKays and Caralyn. Grandparents and other family members sat behind them. Hundreds more gathered outside. The sun shone brightly as it highlighted the fluffy clouds in the blue clear sky. The frail old preacher said a few final words in a barely audible voice.

After shaking hands with family for a half hour, Tucker put an arm around his mother's shoulders and asked, "Mom, will you excuse me? Cara and I will be back in a minute. She wants to visit the graves."

"We will cover. Take your time." Mom smiled and patted his hand. "Some of the family already left for the church. Don't take too long or there might not be any food left."

"You could tell them to start without me."

"I will mention it, but I don't think they will."

Tucker and Caralyn walked to her birth parents' graves.

"Do you remember the first time we came here after you realized who they were?" Tucker asked. "You were still a kid."

"I remember, Tuck. I was afraid so you had to hold my hand. Even though I don't remember them at all, I still love them."

"I know you do, Carrie, and I know you love Mom and Dad, too." Tucker put his hands on her shoulders and held her for a moment as he looked up to watch two white doves riding the warm air currents above them. He looked back at the rest of the mourners. "We should get back."

"I'll be there soon, Tuck. I need a minute."

Tucker squeezed her hand and rejoined everyone as Caralyn spent a moment alone with her birth parents and Grandma Florence. She knelt to remove two dandelions from the tall green grass next to the grave marker. Her heart was heavy as she remembered one of the last times she talked to Nancy. She remembered her exact words.

18

"I know you love him, Cara, and always have. I know it hurt when he married me instead of you. Maybe it was because God knew I wouldn't be here long, and Tucker was mine for the time I had left. You have been very patient, and now he is yours. I want you to marry him and have the family we never were able to. I don't know if it works this way, but I'd like to think I will be able to look down from heaven and see you. I'll try to watch over you and Tuck. I will be the sun and rejoice with you when you are happy, and I will be the thunder when your heart aches. I will be the rain when you cry. I want to watch you grow old together. I love you both more than life itself, and I will be waiting for you when your time is through."

Tears streamed down Caralyn's face as she remembered her promise to Nancy. She looked at her birth parents' headstone again and stood up. She turned to face the still gathered crowd and saw Tucker talking to his mom and dad. As she walked toward him, the whistle of a slow moving freight train made an eerie mournful sound.

She laced her fingers with his, saw him watching the train and asked, "What are you thinking?"

"I hate trains."

"We're leaving for the church," Dad said.

"I'll be right there," Tucker said. "Caralyn wants to say goodbye to Beth and Ray."

"We'll wait."

"Thanks for driving down," Caralyn said. "Are you sure you won't stay for the lunch? There will be lots of food. You can stay."

"Thanks, but you know how uncomfortable Ray is here."

"Okay, I gave you the mailbox key, right?"

"Yes, I'll put your mail on the table. Should I check later in the week?"

"If you have time." Caralyn hugged her sister and watched them leave.

19

"Ready?" Tucker asked.

"Yes, I'm sorry for making you wait. They probably won't let anyone eat until you and the Youngs get there."

Four tables of food lined one end of the basement of the Stockton Woods Methodist Church. After the Youngs and McKays arrived, the preacher prayed and announced the immediate family would be served first.

"I guess we get to go first," Tucker said to Caralyn. "After the Youngs since Sandy and Lloyd are already in line."

Caralyn followed Tucker to the line and watched him fill his plate. "You better eat more than that, Tuck. You haven't had much of an appetite lately."

"Neither have you."

"I could stand to lose a few pounds," she said. "Look! Someone made corn souffle."

"I'll eat some of that. Nancy learned to make it."

"I've tried, but it never tastes as good as Mom's."

An hour later Caralyn stood beside Derren and Richard.

"Are you staying in town all week?" Derren asked.

"Yes, I think we'll head back to the city next Saturday. When do you have to get back?" she asked Richard.

"I'm back to the grind Monday morning at six."

"That early?" she asked.

"Ha! My boss told me to take an extra hour off. Otherwise, I'm usually there by five."

"Poor baby. Your social life must be a wreck."

"It would have to improve to be a wreck."

"Did Natalie come back to the church?" Caralyn asked looking around. "I don't see her."

Derren shook his head. "We drove separately, so she could head home after the service. She didn't go to the cemetery."

Caralyn looked up at him. *I wish you'd tell us what's going on between you and Natalie. I know you're struggling.*

"Are you leaving for Chicago today?" she asked Richard.

"I was tempted to stay another night because of the fancy hotel, but I checked out. I'm staying with my parents tonight. Their old couch is better than the bed I slept on last night."

"What time's your flight?" Derren asked.

"I'm flying out of O'Hare at eight Sunday morning." He looked at Caralyn. "Did you eat anything?"

"I ate everything on my plate."

"Yeah, I bet it was loaded, huh?" Richard put a hand on her side. "You have lost weight."

"Do you think so?"

"Definitely. Your face is thinner, but you still look good."

"Thanks. Maybe I lost a few pounds, but it wasn't on purpose," she replied.

"Caralyn, are you going out to the farm Sunday?" Derren asked.

"We haven't talked about it, but it might be a good idea. It will keep Tucker occupied. Are you going to be there?"

"Yes, but only because Natalie needs to see her mother."

"We should go fishing at Grandpa's pond."

Derren snorted. "Obviously, you haven't been there lately."

"Why do you say that?"

He shrugged. "There's not much water left in it. Certainly not enough to go fishing or swimming."

"What about Uncle Alton's lake? I haven't been there since Tuck and Nancy's wedding." She looked at Richard to see if he would comment, but he didn't.

"It's still there, and he added a dock. Davey helped him build it."

Richard grinned and said, "Maybe we could check it out since we got rained on the last time we were there, Caralyn."

She made a face and tried to poke his side. "I'm not camping out with you even if there's no chance of rain."

"I'll pretend I didn't hear that," Derren said.

"Nothing happened," she said as Richard grinned. This time she smacked his arm. "I wasn't going swimming with you no matter how much I drank."

"I think I see someone I know," Derren said. "I'll let you guys sort out your stories."

Caralyn frowned and said, "Richard, I should smack you where it hurts the most."

"Wouldn't matter."

"Hush, and give me a hug. I might not have a chance to say goodbye later."

He hugged her and kissed the top of her head.

"Cara, Melissa was looking for you," Davey said later.

"What did she want?"

"She wanted to ask about living in Chicago."

"Are you guys thinking of moving?"

Davey laughed and shook his head. "Not a chance. She thinks Butler is too big."

"Chicago is like a thousand Butlers strung out together."

"We're thinking of buying a house. This real estate agent I know said there are close to two hundred houses on the market within the county."

"Sounds like the perfect time for you. Make sure you find one with enough bedrooms. Melissa wants a dozen babies."

"No way. I can see three maybe."

"Are you going to show me your apartment sometime?"

"You can come over whenever you want, Cara. Just call so I can make sure we're not home," he teased.

She poked his arm and said, "You better not come to Chicago and expect to stay with me or Tucker and Nancy."

Davey looked at her.

She realized her mistake, looked up at him and felt her lip tremble.

"It's all right, Carrie," Davey said as he held her. "None of us are used to her being gone."

"We have plenty of food in the fridge," Mom said as she inspected it. "A few of these dishes never made it to the tables. I won't have to cook all week."

22

"Mrs. Young was begging people to take food home because they won't be able to eat it before it goes bad," Caralyn said. "Oh look. There's some cherry pie. I'll eat a piece." She walked into the living room. "Tuck, would you like some cherry pie? There's three slices left."

He stood and waved a hand. "Thanks, but I'm not hungry. Would you mind if I crash at Grandma's house tonight? I'd like to be alone."

"I don't mind. I can sleep in her room."

Dad saw the look on his son. "Sweetie, I think he really means alone in the house."

"Oh, I get it. Give me a chance to grab some clothes, and I will stay here tonight. I can sleep here all week if you want."

"Thanks, Cara. I won't stay depressed forever."

Chapter Three

"Caralyn, would you run next door and check on Tucker, please?" Mom asked. "I'm going to make breakfast, and he needs to eat something. He can't continue this way."

"Okay. I wonder if he got any sleep. I tossed and turned until after two," Caralyn answered. "Did you get any sleep?"

Dad shook his head. "Not really, but I did close my eyes and got some rest."

Caralyn walked out of the kitchen, through the utility room, out the back door, down the steps and looked across the yard to Grandma Florence's white, one-story house. *Maybe now will be the time to sell it. I'm old enough now to live there, but I'm not sure if I want to.* She slowly climbed the back porch steps and walked inside. "Tuck, are you awake? Mom's making breakfast, and you have to eat." She passed through the kitchen into the hallway and looked into both bedrooms. "Where are you?"

He cleared his throat and answered, "In here."

She walked into the living room and saw him. "Did you sleep on the couch all night?"

"I sat here, but I didn't really sleep."

"You didn't even get undressed." She sat beside him and held his hand. "I didn't get much sleep either. I doubt if any of us did, but you have to eat to keep up your strength. Nancy would want..."

"Don't go there, Caralyn. I don't want to hear it."

"Sorry. I don't know what to say. I can empathize with you, but I don't know how you feel."

He squeezed her hand. "Sorry. I didn't mean to snap at you."

"I know."

"Somehow I thought God would work a miracle and heal Nancy. I prayed for that every day until... until I didn't need to anymore."

"I prayed for her too. I hadn't prayed for anything since Grandma passed away."

24

"I don't think I did either."

"Now I feel guilty because I think all my prayers were selfish."

"Yeah, I don't know if I believe what the preacher said about God having everything under control. Does that mean God knew she was going to die and didn't do anything about it?"

Caralyn shrugged. "I don't know. It doesn't seem fair God would let scumbags live and take Nancy away."

He leaned back, closed his eyes and said, "One of the guys on the team is a believer, and he tried to explain how bad things happen to good people."

"I heard that from lots of people along with 'she's in a better place.' It was almost enough to make me sick," Caralyn said. "It's difficult to keep secrets, or hide your life, in Stockton Woods. Beth told me she recognized some of the people who came to the wake as the same ones who sold drugs years ago."

"Back in the 80s and 90s the town went through hard times. Jobs were scarce in the whole county and people did what they had to. It was a matter of survival."

"It's better now, right?" She scooted to the edge of the couch and sat on her legs. "I think it's better."

"There are jobs now because of Amazon and the trucking hub outside of Butler. People are building new homes."

Caralyn grinned and said, "Maybe the population of Stockton Woods will reach a thousand soon."

"Without resorting to counting dogs and cats."

"Thanks for lunch, Mom."

"You should eat more than a sandwich, Tuck."

"I'm not hungry. I need to run and see the Youngs. I promised I would visit with their family. Most of them are at the house."

"They are your family, too," Mom said.

"I suppose, but the only time I saw some of them was at the wedding. Nancy wasn't close to her father's side of the family."

"Please let Donna know we are here if they need anything."

25

"I will, Mom."

"Why wasn't Sandy's baby with them yesterday?" Caralyn asked. "They had him at the wake."

"I don't think they wanted him to be a distraction," Tucker answered. "I will eat with them, so don't wait for me at supper."

"I will stay here tonight, Tuck. You can have the house to yourself again."

"What are you doing? I need to get out of the house." Caralyn asked a few minutes later.

Davey looked at his phone and grinned. "Who is this? Do I know you? I don't answer crank calls."

"Don't try that crap with me. You've got caller ID. Are you busy?"

"If you call being a couch potato watching the Cardinals getting shut out by the Braves being busy, then, yes. Otherwise, I'm bored."

"Good. I'm coming over, and don't say you're not home."

"Rats. Do you have the address?"

"I have it in my phone, but where is it?"

"It's in St. Louis," he teased.

"Tell me how to get there, or I will tell Melissa about the night you..."

"Turn left at the high school. Three blocks east then turn right. Our building is on the right, and we're the door in the middle. Do you need the number?"

"I have 205."

"That's it. Don't expect me to clean up because you're coming."

"Is Melissa there?"

"It's Saturday. She has to work until six. Are you still coming over?"

"Yeah, I would rather see her, but you can keep me entertained for a few minutes."

"Darn it."

"Tucker, we're so sorry about Nancy," one of the aunts said. "She looked so peaceful."

Tucker took a deep breath. *God, please help me get through this. I know they are family and are suffering like me.* "It was a beautiful ceremony, Mrs. Clifford."

"Now. Now. You have to call me Aunt Charmaine. I'm Donna's youngest sister. Did you know there are eight of us siblings?"

"Nancy often mentioned her numerous aunts and uncles," Tucker said with a forced smile.

"I didn't realize you play basketball for a living. I'm Uncle Thomas, but everyone calls me Junior." Thomas shook Tucker's hand. "I thought you were tall until I saw one of your teammates. He was a giant. He must bump his head a lot."

Mr. Young came to his rescue. "You should come outside, Tuck. We're sitting on the patio and talking about crops and how to improve yield. Sounds interesting, huh?" he asked with a wink.

"Mom grew up on a farm, so I get it."

Caralyn knocked on the door. "I know you're in there, Davey. Let me in."

He opened the door and said, "We're not buying anything. I don't care if it's free."

She pushed him to the side and scooted into the apartment. "You could have said yours is the one with the purple door." She looked around the small area.

"The doors are painted bright colors so people can find the right one late at night. I told you I wasn't cleaning up."

"It's not too bad. I've seen worse. The guys' apartment at school was sometimes covered in pizza boxes."

"Yeah, I was there a few times, and it was always pretty clean."

"Only because I cleaned up after them."

"Do you want to see the bedroom and stuff?" Davey asked.

"Not really." She plopped onto the couch. "Are the Cardinals still losing?"

He sat at the other end. "They're down by seven. Doesn't look good."

She leaned back and spread her arms along the top of the couch. "I rarely watch baseball on TV. I'd rather watch it in person." Then she turned her body to face him.

He glanced at her legs then her shorts.

"What are you looking at?"

"Nothing. Sorry for staring, Cara."

"It's okay. Didn't you get any last night? Are you horny?"

"Do you have to be so crass?"

"Did you?"

"No, not that it should matter to you."

She sighed and said, "I haven't had sex for a hundred years. I might as well be a virgin."

"What am I supposed to do about it? I'm your cousin."

"Second cousin if you want to be accurate. Second cousins can get married in some states." She raised one knee and rested her chin on it.

"In case you've forgotten, I'm married to Melissa." He turned off the TV. "We could see if there are any games going on. Teams play at the high school and the diamond by the pool."

"Sounds better than hanging out here. Can we walk, or should I drive."

"I worked all week. You can be the chauffeur."

She drove to the pool.

"It looks like a Little League game. Wanna watch from the car or in the stands?" she asked.

"The bleachers."

They climbed to the top row. She sat close enough for their hips to touch.

"When was the last time you had sex?" he asked.

"When I went to Oregon to see Trent. That was in 2009."

"Then it's only been a year and a half."

"It feels a lot longer," she whispered. "I haven't thought about it very often since Nancy got sick."

"That's understandable."

28

She moved his hand to her left hip and leaned closer to him.

"You broke up because he lives in Oregon, right?"

"I couldn't move there."

"Do you still talk to him?"

"It's been a while. I could call him and see if he's in a relationship."

"Would it make a difference if he is?" He moved his hand to the small of her back.

"Of course. I wouldn't want him to cheat. If I didn't care about that, I could sleep with you and not be so horny."

"Good thing you have morals."

"Hey! That kid hit a homerun."

"He looks bigger than the other players. He must be on steroids."

"Get out! Why would you say that?"

He shrugged.

"Wanna go swimming?"

He looked at the pool. "I think it's only open for kids this afternoon, and I left my trunks at the apartment."

"I didn't mean at the pool. Let's go to Uncle Alton's lake. We can swim, and then I can work on my tan."

"Did you bring a suit?" he asked.

"No, but why would I need one?" she teased.

He moved a few inches away. "I can't do that. Melissa wouldn't understand."

"I was joking. I brought a suit in case I decided to go by myself later."

"You aren't supposed to go swimming alone."

"Yeah, I know. I've got a blanket, sunscreen and... Shoot! I forgot water. Bottled water."

The game ended, and they walked back to her car.

"If you want to go to the lake, I'll go with you. You can work on your tan, and I can do some fishing. Uncle Alton keeps it stocked now."

"Will Melissa be upset since she's stuck at the salon?"

29

"She won't mind if I go fishing."

"I know enough about fishing to know you can't catch anything in the mid-afternoon sun."

"Yeah, but fishing isn't always about catching a fish," he said and she understood.

"Tucker, what are your plans for the next season? Do you have to sign a new contract?" Allan Young asked.

Tucker looked at the youngest of the Young siblings. "I'm signed for two more years. Guaranteed money."

"What do you do to stay in shape during the off-season?" Robert Clifford asked.

Dennis Chapman, one of Mrs. Young's brothers, asked, "How do you deal with the travel? I work for Connecticut Life, and I travel two or three weeks a month."

"It gets old living out of a suitcase, but it's my career." He looked at Mr. Clifford. "I run more than anything. We have a strength and conditioning coach. He sets a program for each player. Some are more conscientious about their training than others."

"It shows. There was a player on the Celtics last year who could barely get up and down the court without huffing and puffing."

"What are you men talking about?" Sandy asked as she carried her baby. Lloyd followed.

Mr. Young stood up, walked over to Sandy and took Lee Andrew from her. "How's my first grandson doing?"

The baby cooed and smiled.

Tucker stared at the ground.

Caralyn changed in the bathroom while Davey used the bedroom.

"I put on trunks in case I change my mind," he said. "My gear is in the closet. I'll grab it and we can go."

"Have you got any bottled water?"

"In the fridge. Grab several. There's a small cooler on top."

30

"I see it."

She drove to the lake.

"That's where his old shed used to be," Davey said.

"I remember the storm that blew off part of the roof. I loved climbing on top and watching the stars or the sunset. He should build a new one."

Davey shrugged. "He doesn't raise cattle anymore. Why would he need it?"

"For me to climb on, silly."

"You're a goof, Cara."

They walked over the hill and she set her blanket close to the edge of the water on the north side. "The ground's flatter here."

Davey set the cooler beside her. "I'm going to fish from the dock. I don't expect to catch anything, but who knows?"

Caralyn removed her shorts and t-shirt, covered herself with sunscreen and lay on the blanket.

"Don't forget to turn over once in a while," he said walking away.

"I know how to keep from getting burned, twerp brain."

"That's a new one. Did you just think of it?"

He sat on the dock for forty minutes before getting bored. He packed up his gear and walked back to where she was laying on her blanket.

"When did you take off your top?"

"Five minutes ago. My back feels red. Is it?" She sat up with her back to him.

"Maybe a little." He sat beside her and removed his t-shirt.

She added sunscreen, held her top to her chest and moved onto her back. "Any luck?"

"A couple nibbles, but I was more interested in clearing my mind."

"What mind?"

"You should write this stuff down, Cara. It's better than TV."

"Shut up, twerp and close your eyes."

31

Tucker pulled into the driveway and hopped out. Caralyn parked behind him a few seconds later.

He watched her get out. "Where have you been?"

"With Davey and Melissa. I went to see him after you left. I checked out their apartment, and we watched a game by the pool. Davey and I went to the lake after that. Melissa had to work until six. When she got home, we ordered a pizza and went back to the lake."

"Did you go swimming?" He waited for her.

"I brought a suit, Tuck."

"I didn't think Davey liked to swim."

"He doesn't, but Melissa does. We swam for a while then sat on the dock with Davey."

"What did you do?" Tucker stuffed his hands in his pockets. "You don't have to answer it's too personal."

"We talked about growing up in Stockton Woods, or out in the country like Davey and Derren. I told Melissa about some of the things Davey and I did when we were kids. She liked hearing the stories because he gets embarrassed."

"I had to listen to Nancy's aunts, uncles, grandparents, old neighbors and other people who knew her one way or another. I'm exhausted. Would you tell Mom and Dad good night for me, please?"

"Of course. Maybe we can do something tomorrow, Tuck."

"It's Sunday, and I'm going to church. You can come with me if you want. Mom and Dad are going."

"I might if I get up in time."

Chapter Four

"We're leaving for church in fifteen minutes, Cara. Are you going with?" Mom asked from outside the bedroom door.

Caralyn jumped out of bed. "I'll go, but I need ten minutes to shower and dress. Can you wait?"

"We can wait, sweetie, but please hurry."

Tucker walked in the back door a couple minutes later. "Is she ready?"

"She's hurrying. Are you going to drive, or should your father?"

"I can drive if you don't mind going in the Jeep," he replied.

"We can take our car," Dad said. "Your mother doesn't like riding in the Jeep, but she will never tell you."

Caralyn dashed out of the bedroom. "Is it all right if I wear jeans? I only brought two dresses, and they're both black."

"Jeans are fine. The church is more casual now. Only your father and the other *old guys* wear suits."

"I like to look professional," Dad said.

"I'll drive," Tucker said and Dad tossed him the keys.

He parked in the street, and they entered through the east doors.

"I'm surprised to see you, Tucker," the greeter said. "But I'm glad you are here."

"Thanks," Tucker said with a half smile.

"Have they remodeled the sanctuary?" Caralyn asked as they settled in the back row.

"They painted the walls, refinished the pews and added the padding. They used to be wood and rather uncomfortable. They're better now."

Caralyn turned and looked at the windows behind her. "I used to stare at the stained glass when I was a kid. I couldn't understand how it was made."

Tucker nodded to Mr. and Mrs. Young. The family took up two entire pews.

"Is the preacher going to mention Nancy?" Caralyn asked.

"I don't know, but I hope he doesn't," he replied.

Before he started the message, the frail preacher mentioned the funeral.

"He's the same preacher from when we were kids, right?" Caralyn asked.

Tucker nodded. "He's been here close to forty years."

Caralyn glanced around the wide sanctuary, saw a few people she remembered, but many more who were unfamiliar.

"Tuck, whenever I come back to this church, I always feel like a kid and kinda like your sister."

"It's not easy to create an adult identity in a church you've grown up in. That's why so many young couples move away."

After the service ended, many of the people wanted to talk to Tucker.

"You can go on out to the farm," he said handing his father the keys. "I'll walk home and get the Jeep."

"We could wait if you'd like," Dad offered.

"No, it might be a while, and Grandma likes to serve dinner on time."

"Cara, are you coming with us?" Mom asked.

"No, I want to wait and ride with Tuck if that's okay."

Mom nodded then waved at Mrs. Boyd. "Okay, but try to hurry him along. He will stay as long as people want to talk to him."

Tucker eventually made his way outside, but was approached by members of Nancy's family.

"I understand it's a tradition for your family to eat Sunday dinner at the Stanfield farm, but would you have time to stop by the house after you eat? Most of the family is leaving this afternoon or evening."

"I will make an effort to drop by before it gets too late, Mr. Young."

He patted Tucker's back. "I appreciate it, son."

Caralyn walked beside him as they crossed the street to head home.

"Are you glad that's over?" she asked.

"Certainly."

They walked a block in silence.

"We used to walk home from church a lot when we were kids. Do you remember going to Summer Bible School?" she asked.

"Yes, and they called it Vacation Bible School."

"Whatever." Caralyn grinned. "We would memorize Bible verses to win a prize, and I would try to beat you."

"I remember one time when I was riding my bike home. I remember starting down this hill, but the next thing I knew was on the side of the road all scratched up."

"I remember. You crashed for some reason, and Mrs. Boyd found you and brought you home."

"I'm going to change into something more comfortable," Tucker said as they reached the house.

"I will too."

She changed into shorts and a t-shirt. Tucker wore faded jeans and a polo shirt with the Bulls' logo.

They were the last to arrive at the farm.

"About time you got here," Uncle Carlton teased. "We were going to start without you."

"It looks like you did," Caralyn said pointing to his plate.

"Tucker, I saved a seat for you in the little room," Grandma said. "There's a place for you, too, sweetie." Grandma brushed a curl from Caralyn's eyes. "Your mother said you went to church. I'm glad."

"I thought I should. It's been a while since I did."

The *little room* was next to the kitchen with a round table large enough for six. It was the place where the kids would eat in prior years. Now Caralyn, the youngest grandchild, was an adult.

Davey put a hand on Tucker's shoulder and said, "Derren wanted me to tell you he tried to talk Natalie into coming, but she absolutely refused. He said he's sorry."

"It's okay. I know he and Natalie are struggling."

35

Later, Tucker carried his plate into the kitchen where Caralyn was helping Mom do the dishes.

"Did you get enough mashed potatoes?" Caralyn asked.

"Yes, but I didn't eat as much as Davey." He snapped a towel at her backside.

"Watch it, bucko," she said with a grin. "These shorts are kinda thin."

"I need to head into town. I promised to say goodbye."

"Okay, but say goodbye to Grandma and Grandpa first."

"I will. Can you ride home with Mom and Dad."

"Sure, unless Davey gives me a ride."

"I hate to eat and run, Grandma, but I need to go into town to say goodbye to Nancy's family. They're heading home today."

Grandma pulled his face to her level and kissed his cheek. "I understand. You can come by the farm later and spend as much time here as you want. Sometimes doing a little work can take your mind off your sorrows."

"Thank you," he whispered giving her a tender hug.

"Cara, would you like to go for a walk?" Davey asked.

"Okay, is Melissa coming?"

"No. She needs to stop by her parents' house. Martha and her husband drove up from Atlanta last night, and she wants to see them and the baby."

"I didn't know she had the baby already."

"A couple months ago, Cara. You've been kinda preoccupied with other things lately."

"I guess. Where are we going?"

"Let's check Grandpa's pond. Dad hired a guy to work on it. It had filled up with so much silt over the years. Dad wanted it to be a real pond again."

They walked around the barn, and he opened the gate for her.

She grinned and said, "Thanks. I thought you would make me crawl over like I used to."

"Maybe I don't think of you as a tomboy anymore."

36

They walked through the orchard along a well-worn path.

"Do you ever think about what will happen to the farm after Grandma and Grandpa are gone?"

"Yeah, and I've talked to Dad and Uncle Alton about it."

"What do they want to do?"

"Since they already have their own farms, they want to sell it."

"No!" She punched his shoulder. "How could they do that? Grandpa built it from scratch. He would hate the idea."

"So true." Davey grinned and added, "That's why they've agreed to sell it to me."

She stopped walking and looked at him. "For real?"

He stopped, turned around and smiled. "Totally serious, Cara. We've been putting money aside for a down payment."

"Good, but I hope it's several years before you buy it."

"No one wants Grandma and Grandpa to move."

"I wasn't thinking about moving, Davey. They are getting close to their nineties."

"I get it, but they're in good health."

They reached the pond and sat on the south side in the new sand.

"Anything can happen. When you do buy it, will you make many changes?"

"I might update the house, but I don't plan to build a new one."

"It's inevitable there will be a new house on this spot. Your father built a new house."

"When I was like two." He moved onto his back with his knees in the air and stuck a shoot of wild dill in his mouth.

She lay on her side next to him. "Uncle Alton replaced the old house where Ed and Duane grew up."

"I have no memory of it, but I've heard stories. It once belonged to Grandma's brother. I can't remember his name. Did you know Grandma is the youngest sibling."

"She might have told me, but I don't have a clear memory of meeting any of her brothers and sisters."

37

"Me either. She's the only one left, and Grandpa's only brother died when we were little kids."

Caralyn moved onto her back, lifted her knees and rested her leg against his.

"I feel so bad for Derren," she said. "Does he talk to you much? He rarely talks to Tucker anymore."

"I call him once in a while, but he never initiates the call."

"His situation has changed so much since he married Natalie."

Davey shifted onto his side and touched a small scar on her leg. "How's your friend Richard doing? I saw him, but didn't have a chance to talk."

"He's working too many hours. His social life is in the toilet, and he was one of those guys with a different girlfriend every week."

He stared at her until she noticed.

"What?" She realized what he wanted to know. "Never happened. Close once or twice, but no cigar for that boy." Then she smacked his thigh hard.

"Ow! What was that for?"

"My feet don't smell, you twerp."

He laughed and looked at her sneakers. "Would you like a foot massage? I've been practicing on Melissa."

"No, and I don't want to hear anything about what you guys have been practicing."

"Not even safe sex?"

She flipped onto her stomach with her feet in the air. "Do you mean you're using birth control?"

"No, but we aren't having sex in dangerous places," he teased.

Tucker parked on the street three houses down from the Young home because that was as close as he could get. He stuck his hands in his pockets and walked to the front door. He wondered if he should ring the bell or walk right in. He didn't have to decide because Dennis Chapman opened it and stepped outside.

"I'd run if I were you."

"Why?" Tucker asked the balding, rotund man.

"It's a zoo in there. Everyone wants to hold Lee Andrew, and he's fussing. Charmaine is getting on Donna's nerves and my brothers are arguing about baseball."

Tucker could hear the commotion inside and sighed. "I promised to stop by for a bit. I have to keep my word."

Dennis clapped Tucker on the back. "Good luck."

Tucker stepped inside without being noticed. He saw Mr. Young sitting in his favorite chair and nodded.

Mr. Young stood up and shepherded Tucker into the kitchen. "I bet it's not like this at the Stanfield house."

"There aren't as many people, and they're pretty quiet."

"You don't have to stay long, and I don't expect you to say goodbye to everyone. I'm honored you came."

Tucker smiled and said, "I feel privileged to be part of your family, Mr. Young."

Tucker escaped two hours later. He hurried to his Jeep, got in and took off. He was about to turn left onto the highway to head to the farm, but hesitated. He turned right and then made a quick left and drove to the cemetery. He parked close to Nancy's grave. He listened for the sound of a train, but heard only the chattering of birds and the wind whistling through the trees. He slowly made his way to the fresh mound of dirt and sat in the grass. He picked a yellow dandelion and pulled at the flowered head. He glanced around to make sure he was alone, and then whispered, "I miss you so much already. How will I survive without you? I know you told me not to grieve over you, but how can I not?"

Caralyn and Davey walked onto the front porch where Grandma and Grandpa were sitting in their metal rockers.

"Where have you been, child?" Grandma asked.

"We went for a walk and ended up at the pond," Davey answered.

Grandma's eyes sparkled.

"There you are," Mom said coming out the front door. "We were going into Butler. Would you like to come with or go home?"

Caralyn looked at Davey. "Could you give me a ride into town?"

"Sure."

"I'll pass on Butler. I know you're going to see Dad's boss. He's boring and is always making jokes about the college."

"I wish I could skip out, but I have to show support for your father. If you see Tucker, tell him we will be home by nine."

She and Davey left a few minutes later. They got to the house, but didn't see the Jeep in either driveway.

"Maybe the Jeep's in the garage at his house or your house. How do you keep track of who lives where?"

Caralyn pointed. "That's Grandma's house. I live there now. Tucker lives in the McKay house when he's home unless he and Nancy are staying..." She teared up. "I did it again, didn't I?"

"It will take some time to get used to her being gone. It's not your fault, Cara." He looked at both houses. "Do you have any idea where he might have gone?"

She thought about it and snapped her fingers. "Yes, I bet he's at the cemetery. Take me there, please."

They jumped back into Davey's pickup and drove to the Lincoln Ridge cemetery.

"Slow down." She pointed. "There's the Jeep. Drop me off here, Davey. Thanks for the ride."

Caralyn saw Tucker sitting in the grass next to Nancy's grave. He didn't hear her and jumped when she sat on her knees behind him and put her hands on his shoulders.

"Carrie, why are you here?"

"Mom... No, all of us were worried about you. Have you been here long?"

He shrugged and said, "An hour maybe. I can't remember. I stopped at the Youngs to say goodbye then came here. I was talking to Nancy. Does that sound silly?"

"Not at all, Bubby." She scooted beside him.

He leaned against her and smiled.

40

Chapter Five

"Drive carefully, son," Mom said as Tucker got into his Jeep. "Caralyn, keep an eye on him and make him pull over if he gets sleepy."

"I'll drive if he needs a break, Mom." She hugged her parents and climbed into the passenger seat. "I will call when we get home."

Tucker waved, looked over his shoulder and backed out of the driveway. He put the Jeep in gear, waved again and drove away.

"Did it sound weird to say I'd call when we got home? Stockton Woods is still our real home," Caralyn said.

"I'm not sure I can think of it as home anymore, but Chicago won't feel like home without her there."

"Nothing has felt real for the last six months. You weren't even married for a whole year."

"Please don't remind me, okay?"

After four and a half hours on the road, Tucker parked the Jeep in the garage.

"Thanks for the ride," Caralyn said as she tugged on her suitcase in the rear.

"Let me help you with that, Cara." He lifted it out and set it on the floor. "I'm sorry for being a grump on the way home, but I didn't feel like making small talk."

"It's okay, Tuck. I didn't feel like talking much either. We didn't talk much at all this last week. We hardly saw each other after I found you at the cemetery. You ran a hundred miles a day to get in shape."

He grinned and said, "It wasn't that far."

"I spent more time with Davey and Melissa than anyone."

Tucker stared at her. "I heard it was mostly Davey. Not Melissa."

"She was working, and he was on vacation, or he took personal days. Whatever. We've always been close."

41

He pulled his duffel bag out, closed the Jeep and headed inside. He punched the button to close the garage door and waited for Caralyn.

"I'm sorry for getting on your case about Davey. Nancy wasn't too fond of him, so I don't talk to him that much. I don't talk to Derren very often anymore, either. We aren't in college, and we have different lives."

"Did you expect it to stay the same?"

"In a way. I thought we'd always be close. Hasn't worked out like that."

"We're still close, aren't we?" she asked opening the door to the rear of the hallway.

"Yes, but we live together."

She grinned.

"I meant in the same building."

"Yes, but the last few months have been weird. I've stayed in your apartment almost as much as my own." She walked to the mailboxes before remembering she gave her key to Beth.

"I appreciate how you sacrificed your life to take care of Nancy the way you did."

"I missed a few classes, but you have a career." She stopped and he almost walked into her. "Are you feeling guilty because you didn't drop everything to spend twenty-four hours a day with her?"

"No."

"Bull! I know you, Tucker McKay. You are thinking things would have turned out differently had you quit your career and spent every hour with her. Trust me, bucko, it wouldn't have mattered."

They didn't speak again as they climbed the stairs.

Caralyn stopped at her floor and asked, "Do you want to order something for dinner? My fridge is empty, and you never have food in yours."

"Sure. Order whatever you want and call me. I'll come down and eat with you."

"I could have it delivered to your place."

He shook his head. "No. I'll come downstairs. My place is a mess."

She ordered a deep dish supreme pizza from the place two blocks over and called him when it arrived.

"Be right there. I'm throwing a load of laundry in the washer. What setting should I do her underwear on?"

"Tuck, it won't matter now," she answered.

He took a deep breath. "Yeah, I guess you're right." He threw them in with his load and turned on the washer. "Be right there. Go ahead and start if you want."

When he wasn't there thirty minutes later, she called.

"Sorry, I got busy going over bills. Is there any left?"

"I didn't eat it all. I'll bring it up."

"No. I will come down now." He ended the call and looked around the unkempt apartment. He shook his head, grabbed his keys and dashed downstairs.

"Sorry, I got busy and lost track of time."

"Yeah, that's what you said when I called. I put it in the oven to stay warm. Should I fix a plate for you?"

"I'll do it."

He sat at the table across from her.

"Would you like my help going through Nancy's clothes?"

He took a bite and thought about her offer. "I'm not ready to start. Maybe in a few weeks."

"How are you going to keep busy now? For the last six months, you've been taking care of her. She's gone, and you have a tremendous void in your life."

"Do you think I'm unaware of my circumstances, Caralyn?" he asked sharply.

"Of course not, but I think you are determined to isolate yourself from everyone."

"I'm the one who suffered the loss."

She shook her head. "That's crap! Sure, you suffered the loss of your wife, but everyone who knew Nancy is suffering from her loss."

43

"Not like me," he said.

She cut a slice of the pizza in half and rejoined him. "Of course not, but you're acting like you're the only one grieving for her. That just isn't the case."

He stared at her for a moment. "Are you finished with your lecture, Professor Dawson?"

"No! I have one other thing to get on your case about."

"What?"

"When was the last time you cleaned the apartment? I know that's why you don't want me up there. You're ashamed of how cluttered and raunchy it probably is."

"I've been busy."

"No doubt, but now's the time to start putting your life back together. I am not going to let you sulk and mope around looking like you just lost your best friend..."

"Caralyn."

"Sorry, I was thinking about a pet dog. You have lost a very close friend, but you still have me to pester you and make your life miserable," she said with a grin.

"Hey. I'm going to church this morning. Want to go with?" Tucker asked.

Caralyn looked at the time. "How soon are you leaving?"

"Thirty minutes. It starts at ten thirty, and we have to drive." He opened the fridge and pulled out the milk. He sniffed it and dumped it in the sink.

"Where is this church? There's one down the block."

He closed the fridge door. "It's in Westbrook Glen."

"Where's that? I've never heard of that neighborhood."

"It's not in the city. It's a suburb and it's not a Methodist church."

"What is it? It's not some weird cult is it?" she asked with a giggle. "Have you been brainwashed like Jeremiah did to me?"

"No, you brat. It's a Nazarene church. Not a cult."

"Never heard of it. Why do you want to go there when there's a Methodist church within walking distance?"

"I met the pastor, and I like him. He's a little older than us..."

"You're only twenty-four. Did I wish you a happy birthday? I can't remember."

"My birthday's in April."

"I know. Can't you tell when I'm teasing anymore?"

"Not always. Be ready in thirty if you want to go."

When they arrived at the church, the parking lot was almost completely full.

"There's a spot next to that Prius, Tuck. I don't think you're going to get any closer." She looked at the building and the small parking lot. "How big is this church?"

"You don't mean the building, right?" He pulled in next to the blue Prius.

"I can see the building. How many people attend here?"

He shrugged, turned off the Jeep and got out. "Maybe a hundred. One twenty tops."

"That's bigger than Stockton Woods Methodist."

"That church is dying because none of our generation sticks around. This church is full of young people, and they have a great band."

"You mean like a real band and not a bunch of amateurs who can't sing on key?"

"I don't know anything about singing on key, but I like the music they play."

"How long have you been coming here? You never told me about it."

"The first time I came here was in April."

"Why? How did you hear about it?" she asked as Tucker opened the door for her.

She was startled when someone said, "Good morning. Welcome to Westbrook Glen Nazarene. It's good to see you."

Tucker shook hands with the man and Caralyn smiled.

"Who was that?" she asked after they entered the main sanctuary.

45

"Not sure."

"Why did he act so excited to see us? He doesn't have a clue who I am."

"I don't remember his name, but every time I've come here, there's been someone at the door to welcome me."

"What did he give you?"

"It's called the Guide. It lists all the activities during the week."

Caralyn snatched it away from Tucker. "The only thing our church back home had during the week was when there were enough teens to have a mid-week meeting."

"Yeah, this is different. They have small groups that meet to do stuff." He smiled at a family and they waved back.

"Do people recognize you?" she asked then smiled at an older couple. *They definitely aren't our age.*

"We can sit here, Carrie." He pointed to screens on either side of the stage. "Those are announcements about what's coming up."

A few minutes later a man walked out on stage and welcomed everyone before praying.

"Is that the pastor you met?" Caralyn asked softly.

Tucker nodded.

"What's his name?"

"Aaron Duncan."

Caralyn closed her eyes and listened patiently. While Pastor Duncan prayed, a band came out on stage. As he finished, the band began playing.

Tucker was approached by several boys after the service. He spent time talking to them before he and Caralyn were finally able to head toward the door.

"It was good to see you again, Tucker."

"It was good to be back, Pastor Duncan," Tucker said shaking hands with the slender man.

Pastor Duncan turned, smiled and said, "You must be Caralyn Dawson."

"I must," she answered with a giggle. *I've never been to a church with a young preacher. You can't be thirty.*

"Tucker has told me how you helped during Nancy's illness and her passing. I also know you've grown up together," Pastor Duncan said.

"I loved the band," Caralyn said. She looked up at Tucker. *How much have you told him?*

"We are fortunate to have so many talented and dedicated musicians in our congregation. We aren't a megachurch by any means."

"I will email you later, Pastor Duncan. I have some questions about the scripture passage you used."

"Please call me Aaron. It feels weird to have people call me Pastor Duncan like I'm some old man."

Caralyn grinned and followed Tucker. She looked back over her shoulder at the handsome preacher.

"Where should we go for lunch?" Caralyn asked as they got in Tucker's Jeep. "There must be plenty of places to choose from out in the boonies."

"The boonies?" Tucker laughed. "We're from Stockton Woods, remember?"

"I was kidding. I've seen every chain of fast-food places imaginable on this road."

"Should we stop and get something to take home?"

"We could, but what about a picnic?" she asked. "We just passed a park, and I saw a few tables."

"Okay, but you have to buy. I put all my money in the offering."

She smacked his arm. "Tell me you didn't."

He laughed and answered, "I wrote a check."

"Let's get something from there." She pointed to a fast-food shop with a large hot dog on the roof. "It looks like a local place. Maybe it's like The Curve."

"I've never eaten there, but we can try it. If it's good, we could grab something on Sundays since we'll be in the area."

"Do you plan to keep going to that church?" she asked.

He pulled up to the red light, waited to make a right turn and drove around the block.

"The entrance is right there, Tuck. Let's park and go inside. I want to smell the food before we order anything."

He laughed, parked the Jeep and said, "Are you going to walk into the kitchen and do an inspection?"

She jumped out and said, "No, but you can get a feel for a place by how good it smells. The food, I mean."

"Is that why we never sat inside at The Curve?"

She hurried to catch up with him. "We would eat inside once in a while, but it was more fun to sit outside." She scooted past him as he opened the door.

They checked out the handwritten menu behind the counter.

A teenage girl with a sincere smile and a paper cap with the name Bozo's Dogs asked, "What can I get for you?"

"Go ahead, Tuck. I'm still trying to decide," Caralyn said.

"I would like the number five," Tucker said.

"What's that?" Caralyn asked.

He pointed and said, "A burger, fries and a drink. Nothing unusual."

She leaned against Tucker, chewed her lip and said, "I would like a hot dog, fries, a Coke and onion rings, please." She looked at Tucker. "You're buying, right?"

"You are such a spoiled brat, Cara."

They took the food to the park.

"This table's clean and it's in the shade." She set her Coke on the table and sat on the bench facing the street. "The food smells delicious."

Tucker sat across from her and opened the bag.

"Are you going to share the onion rings?"

"No, you should have bought your own." She took a sip of Coke then grabbed a fry.

"Technically, I did buy them."

She waved and said, "Fine. You can try one."

They were quiet as they ate. Caralyn watched two kids playing on the playground equipment, then looked at Tucker.

"What?" he asked and then swiped a second onion ring.

"How did you meet that preacher? Did you already tell me?"

"Alphonso told me about the church."

"Alphonso from the Bulls?"

Tucker laughed. "I don't know any other Alphonso. The burger is good. How's your dog?"

She shrugged. "It's a dog. You can have the pickle, but I like the onions." She grabbed the last onion ring. "Tell me more about Pastor Aaron."

He looked at her and saw her smile. "He's married."

She looked away. "So what? I don't care about that."

He laughed. "I saw you checking him out."

"He is rather handsome for a preacher."

"Are preachers not allowed to be handsome?"

"Every one I've ever seen was old and looked like they just swallowed a dill pickle. He seemed happy and kinda normal."

"I'll tell him..."

"Don't you dare!" She swatted his hand. "How much have you told him about us?"

"Don't worry. I haven't told him what a delinquent you are."

She glared at him. "I'm serious."

"Be real. I didn't tell him anything about that."

Chapter Six

"Let me in, Tucker James! I know you're home," Caralyn shouted after banging on the door several times. She listened and finally heard footsteps and then the deadbolt being turned.

He opened the door and stood in the doorway. "I'm busy."

"No you're not." She ducked under his arm, but he grabbed her around the waist. "Let me go, dweeb brain."

He let go and she scampered past him.

"Why haven't you answered your phone? It goes straight to voicemail."

"I turned it off. What do you want, Caralyn?" He closed the door and picked up an empty bag from McDonald's.

She looked around and placed her hands on her hips. "And I thought Derren and Richard were slobs." She picked up a pizza box and two pieces fell out. "At least you've eaten sometime in the last few days."

"I don't need a lecture." He walked to the couch and plopped down.

"I'm not here for that. I want to do something. I'll help you clean if you take me somewhere."

"Why?"

"I'm bored." She joined him on the couch then stood up, reached down and picked up a paper plate. "Why take me somewhere, or why would I help you clean up?"

"Either. Neither. I don't care."

She walked into the open kitchen area, saw dirty dishes in the sink and opened the dishwasher. "Are these clean or dirty?" She pulled out a plate. "Never mind. Do you have dishwasher detergent?"

"Under the sink, I think."

"Good grief. Can't you even do your own dishes?"

"You know I can."

She loaded the dishwasher, added detergent and started it. "When was the last time you changed the sheets?" She stared at him. "They probably smell like a locker room."

He shrugged, stood up and opened the fridge. "I need to do some grocery shopping."

She moved past him and peered inside. "No doubt. Is there anything edible in there?"

"Probably not. Will you help me?"

She did an about-face. "You know I will, Tuck. It hurts me to see you like this. I wish I could snap my fingers, or make a wish, or do something to erase your memory."

He touched the tip of her nose. "At least I haven't started drinking or using drugs."

She poked his stomach and said, "You better not, or I will murder you..." She put a hand to her mouth. "Sorry, Bubby."

"It's okay. If you help, I'll clean this place up. Nancy would be furious if she could see it. Then we can go shopping."

"I have a taste for meat loaf and baked beans. I could make it for dinner."

"Do you know how to make cheesy potatoes?"

She shook her head. "Not really, but I could call Mom and get the recipe."

They sat at the counter to eat a few hours later.

"What do you think? Is the meat loaf okay?"

Tucker took another bite, tilted his head back and forth as he chewed, swallowed then said, "It's better than three-week-old fried baloney."

"Then you shouldn't have to eat anymore." She tried to grab his plate, but he grabbed her hand.

"I'll choke it down somehow. Thank you for making it. I haven't had a decent meal in ages."

"There's enough baked beans and cheesy potatoes for tomorrow unless you're still hungry."

"Two helpings was enough. I should have bought some steaks. I could use the grill."

She scraped the last of her potatoes onto her fork and asked, "Have you used it at all this year? Probably not. Silly question."

51

"I can't remember the last time. I'll have to check the propane."

She put their plates in the sink then opened the dishwasher. "I'll put these away if you promise you won't let the dishes pile up in the sink."

"I won't." He looked over his shoulder. "Would you help me change the sheets, please?"

She grinned and whispered, "I remember another time when we changed the sheets."

"I'll put these in the washer," Caralyn said later. "You need to change the sheets once a week. Maybe more often if you go to bed all sweaty."

"Yes, Mom," he teased.

She started the washer and joined him on the couch.

"How many classes do you have left, Cara?"

"Just the one I dropped when Nancy got sick. I'm making it up now. By August I will have my master's degree."

"Have you applied for any jobs?" he asked after picking up the TV remote.

"Don't turn it on," she said. "Let's talk."

He tossed the remote aside. "Okay. You go first."

"How serious are you about that church?"

He leaned back, closed his eyes and said, "It's more than just a church building, Cara."

"I know that."

"The church in Stockton Woods was okay, but I need something more. Something deeper. Until I went there, I never thought much about Jesus other than I knew I should go to church because it's the right thing to do."

"Like you have a checklist of items to get you into heaven, huh?"

"I guess."

"I feel the same way. I stopped going because it felt empty to me. It was like a social club you needed to belong to, or else you wouldn't fit into the proper society. Does that make any sense?"

"It does now."

She turned to face him, tucked her feet under her and held a throw pillow to her chest. "I felt something different at that church. I didn't hear anyone swearing after church."

He laughed and asked, "Why would you say that?"

"There were times back home when we would come out of church and guys would be smoking and cursing about stuff. It was like they went to church, sat through a sermon and now they could do whatever they wanted until the next time they needed a church fix."

He grinned and said, "You used to have a mouth on you that could embarrass a marine."

She threw the pillow at him. "Shut it! I try to watch my language now."

"I imagine every church has people who are more involved, if that's the right word, than others. Some people don't want to get involved because they might need to move out of their comfort zone and dig deeper into a relationship with Jesus."

"Is all this church stuff because of Nancy getting sick, or were you a closet Jesus freak and never told anyone?"

"I think I've always been curious about religion, but never tied it to a real relationship."

"It's difficult to have a relationship with someone who isn't around."

He sat up straighter. "That's just it, Caralyn. Jesus is here. I can tell because I have changed."

"Yeah, you've changed all right."

"Fine. I'll keep the apartment clean from now on." He threw the pillow back to her. "What about a job? Do you still want to work for a publisher?"

"Maybe, but I want to write more. I could get a job as a translator. They make good money, and I can speak three languages."

"Four," he said holding up his fingers.

"What? Oh, right. I can speak American, too," she said in Italian.

53

"You're a goofball, Cara. Have you worked on that romance novel lately?"

"Not in a few months. I should take another look at it."

"You should finish it. It was pretty good for what it was."

"What was it, Tuck? Please tell me." She tried to kick him, but he grabbed her foot.

"You know. One of those sappy stories they make into Hallmark movies."

"I hate you," she said with a grin. "Either let go of my foot or give me a foot massage."

He quickly let go.

"Don't you dare say my feet smell."

"Does your nose run?"

"What?"

"Never mind. Are you spending the night, or should I call you a cab?"

"Ha! Ha! I think I can make it to my apartment under my own power." She stood up, made sure her key was in her pocket and walked to the door. "I will be back to do a surprise inspection. You better make sure you keep this place shipshape."

He stood up and saluted. "What day can I expect your inspection, General Dawson?"

"Do I look stupid? It's a surprise inspection, twerp."

Before she could open the door he raced to her and put his hands on her shoulders. "Thanks for getting on my case, Carrie. I've been feeling sorry for myself and blaming God and everyone I could think of for what happened to Nancy."

She turned around, wrapped her arms around his waist and rested her head on his chest. "It's okay to miss her and think about her, but we have to move on. You know that's what she told you to do."

"I know." He hugged her tighter. "At least I still have you to harass me."

You'll always have me, Bubby.

Chapter Seven

"Are you coming with me, Cara?" Tucker asked Sunday morning.

"I'm ready. Should I come upstairs, or meet you in the garage?" she asked.

"You can come upstairs, General Dawson. I know you want to check the apartment."

"Have you kept it clean?"

He looked around. "Yes. Everything is shipshape."

"Am I a general, or should I be an admiral?"

"You're a goof. Unless you want to wait in the garage, come on up."

She knocked on his door three minutes later. He let her in, and she marched right to the kitchen. "What did you do with all the dirty dishes?"

"I used that fancy machine under the counter. Did you know it's magic?" He used his country bumpkin accent. "You put dirty dishes in there, and press a couple buttons and poof. They come out clean as a whistle."

She shook her head. "Why am I friends with you?"

"Because I'm such a funny guy?"

"You're not funny just weird. Are you ready?"

"Give me a second." He picked up his Bible from the table. "I'm ready."

She pointed to it. "They have some of those at the church. Why do you have to bring your own?"

"I can make notes in mine."

"You aren't supposed to write in a Bible. It's sacred."

"Yes, but Alphonso showed me his. He's got notes all over the margins, some verses are highlighted with a marker and the thing looks like it's falling apart."

"Can't he buy a new one? The Bulls probably pay him more than you since he's a starter."

"Fine. No more free tickets for you. Let's go."

"Are you going to flirt with Pastor Aaron again?" Tucker asked as they pulled into the parking lot.

"I did not flirt with him, Tucker McKay. I said I thought he was handsome."

"He is still married." Tucker parked next to a gray Prius.

"I will slug you after church." She got out and asked, "Does everyone here drive a Prius?"

"I don't."

"Obviously, goof. Are there any single men in the church who might be interested in a gorgeous young lady of taste and sophistication?" she asked batting her eyes.

"Yeah. Do you know where they could find one?"

"Twerp brain. I hate you."

"I'll ask around. Maybe there's a homeless guy with poor eyesight who might be interested."

She put her hands together as if praying. "Oh, please, Tuck. That's more than I could ever hope for."

He shook his head and opened the church door for her. "Don't sit next to me. Find a spot on the other side of the building."

The greeter smiled and said, "Good morning! It's good to see you again..."

Tucker talked to Pastor Duncan after the service while Caralyn waited. She saw a young couple approaching and moved closer to Tucker.

"Hello, I don't think we've met. I'm Claire Halston and this is my husband, Quinn." She offered a hand and Caralyn shook it. "I saw you last week."

"That was my first Sunday. You sing with the band, right?"

"Yes, and Quinn plays guitar. He can't sing a lick, but he tries."

"I thought the band sounded amazing."

"We try our best," Claire said. She looked at her husband then back at Caralyn. "Would you and Tucker be interested in grabbing lunch? We know several places with good food that don't cost an arm and a leg."

"I'd have to ask Tuck." She turned and touched his arm.

Tucker turned and shook hands with Quinn. "I'd love to have lunch. I'm not familiar with the restaurants in the area. We live in the city."

Claire looked at Caralyn's hand, but didn't see a ring.

"I could drive, or you could follow. Whichever works best for you," Quinn said.

Tucker looked at Caralyn. "Do you have a preference?"

"If you drive, we could head home and not need to come back for your Jeep."

"Good idea. I'll follow," Tucker said.

He discussed a couple options with Quinn while Caralyn listened to Claire talk about the church.

"Sounds good. We will follow you, and if we get split up, I have an idea where it's located."

Caralyn slid into the booth ahead of Tucker, smiled and said, "This reminds me of the Jennings Sisters place in Butler."

Claire handed menus to Caralyn and Tucker.

"What do you recommend?" Tucker asked.

"The burgers are great, and they give you a ton of fries," Quinn said.

"I love the chopped salads," Claire said. "I usually take half of it home."

The men ordered burgers, Claire ordered her salad, but Caralyn decided to try the chicken burrito.

"Wow! This is huge," Caralyn said when her burrito arrived. "Tucker, you might have to help me eat this later." She looked at his mound of fries and stole one. "These are good. Will you share?"

"If I must."

Quinn prayed before they started eating.

"How long have you known each other?" Claire asked as she poured dressing on her salad.

Caralyn looked at Tucker and grinned. "I was a baby when I met him."

Claire stared at her for a moment, then smiled and said, "I thought you were dating, but you're brother and sister."

Tucker waved a hand and replied, "Sorry, Claire, but you're wrong on both accounts."

Quinn was busy with his burger, but he listened.

"I don't understand," Claire said.

Tucker explained their backstory. He mentioned Nancy, but didn't dwell on her illness and passing.

"I'm sorry about your wife," Quinn said.

"Thanks," Tucker replied with a nod.

"So, you aren't brother and sister, or even related, but you both call Tucker's parents Mom and Dad. It is maybe... unique."

"When I was a baby, and up to about four or so, I thought Tuck was my brother even though we lived in different houses."

"That was because your grandmother taught school, right?" Quinn asked.

"Yes, and I spent my days at his house and went back home when Grandma got home from teaching in Butler. Mom didn't go back to teaching until I started kindergarten," Caralyn explained. "Mrs. McKay, I mean. Calling her Mom probably confuses you. I don't remember my birth mother at all."

"We live in the same building in Holland Park," Tucker said. "I live on the top floor, and she lives right below me."

"Where did you go to school?" Quinn asked.

"We both graduated from Midwest Central University in New Lebanon," Tucker answered.

"I'm working on my masters at McCormick University." Caralyn grinned and added, "I took real classes. He played basketball and took classes like Advanced Addition for Dummies and Basketball Spinning..."

Tucker put his hand over her mouth. "I have a degree in Sports Management. After my career is over, I would like to coach basketball at the college level." He removed his hand, and she stuck out her tongue.

"He is barely literate. No one knows how he passed his classes," Caralyn said. "Where did you go?"

58

"We met at and graduated from Southeast Nazarene University in Macon, Georgia," Quinn answered. "I grew up in Atlanta, and Claire was born in Taylorville, but moved to Athens when she started school. Grade school."

"What did you study?" Tucker asked.

"Music Ministry. My field was guitar and Claire's was piano. It equipped us to be worship pastors. We also teach school."

"Is that why the church has such a talented band?" Caralyn asked.

"We are fortunate to have dedicated volunteers. Do you sing or play an instrument?" Claire asked.

Tucker grinned and said, "She can play the radio, but can't sing a lick."

"I can sing. Just not very well. I don't have a talent for it."

"What was it like growing up in such a small town?" Quinn asked. "Atlanta is pretty big."

"Tell me," Tucker said. "We fly into Hartsfield-Jackson, and it's huge. Stockton Woods is about a thousand in population..."

Caralyn faked a yawn, and Tucker saw it.

"He asked."

"Yes, but you don't need to give him the history of the town." She looked at Quinn then Claire. "Sometimes I hate living there, but other times I can't see myself living anywhere else."

Eventually, they finished eating and Caralyn asked for a box to take her burrito home.

"I'll get the check," Quinn said. "We asked you guys out, so I should pay. You can grab the check next time."

"Thanks, Quinn. I'll take you up on it."

"If you ever need to talk about Nancy, I have a talent for keeping my mouth shut. There's always Pastor Aaron, too."

Tucker nodded, and they headed out to the cars.

"That's me over there," Quinn said pointing to a white Prius.

Caralyn nudged Tucker and whispered, "What did I tell you?"

"It was nice to meet you, Caralyn," Claire said. "I hope to see you again real soon."

Tucker stood behind Caralyn and put his hands on her shoulders. "I'll try to drag the delinquent to church, but she likes to be lazy sometimes."

"I do not," she said. "I keep busy, but during the off-season, he doesn't do anything but eat and get fat."

Tucker squeezed her shoulders. "She's partly right."

"Have a good week," Claire said.

Tucker opened the Jeep and they got in.

"Why are you looking at me like that?" she asked.

"Because I was going to smack your bottom for calling me fat, but then I realized it might not look proper."

"I don't think they would have cared."

Quinn drove away and Claire looked over her shoulder at Tucker's Jeep.

"What?" Quinn asked.

"I got the feeling they're more than old friends. Did you?"

"Why would you think that? He explained their familial relationship. She was an orphan, and his family adopted her."

"Why do they live together?"

Quinn turned right at the light. "They live in the same building. Not the same apartment."

"That's still pretty close. Holland park is an expensive neighborhood. I know he plays basketball, but how can she afford an apartment and go to school at the same time?"

Quinn laughed and said, "That sounds like a case for Snoop Halston. The wannabe private investigator."

Chapter Eight

"We're coming home Monday," Tucker said. "Why do you need two suitcases?"

"They aren't filled all the way," she answered. "I might want to bring more clothes to Chicago."

"You mean you still have clothes at home?" He grabbed one of the cases and lifted it. "No books or bricks."

She pulled the other one down the stairs and to the garage. He tossed his duffel bag and her cases in the back of the Jeep.

She climbed in and asked, "Could we stop at Nico's? I crave one of their beef sandwiches."

He lifted an eyebrow and looked at her.

"No! I'm not pregnant. Impossible if you get my drift."

"Didn't think so."

"Did you tell Pastor Aaron we weren't going to be at church tomorrow?"

"Yeah. I told him we were going home for the holiday."

She switched on the radio. "What station is this?"

"It's a Christian college station on the North Side. Don't you like it?" He backed out and hit the remote to close the garage.

"I'll give it a try."

"We won't be able to pick it up for long. It's not real powerful."

They listened to the station until it faded into static south of the city.

"What did you think?" Tucker asked.

She switched to a classic rock station. "It was okay, but I don't know the songs. I can sing along to these." She started to sing as off-key as she could.

"Who's strangling a cat?"

She grinned and asked, "Don't you like my singing? I think I'll try out for the worship band."

"Please don't."

"I'm joking. I wouldn't have the courage to get on the stage in front of everyone like the singer's wife from Fridays At Five."

61

"Her name's Emmy and she has a bunch of CDs out. The worship band sang one last Sunday."

"For real?"

"Lots of churches sing her songs according to Quinn."

"Who's in charge of the worship band? Is it Quinn or Claire?"

"No, it's the other guitar player. His name's Jacob Baxter, I think. I haven't met him."

"Are we going to eat inside, or take it to go?" Tucker asked after they exited the Interstate and drove into New Lebanon.

"We're making good time. Let's eat inside. I could use a break. You should buy something that doesn't bounce you all around."

"But it's great off-road and going through snow," he said.

"The only off-roading you've ever done was to drive down to the bottoms of Jones' corner, and that field isn't exactly rough terrain."

"I've driven through snow."

They parked at Nico's and went inside. She stopped, closed her eyes and took a deep breath.

"What are you doing, Cara? People will run you over if you stand there."

"I was taking in the aroma of grease and beef. Will you order for us while I use the restroom and grab a booth."

He rolled his eyes. "You've used that excuse a thousand times. You don't want to pay."

"Why should I when I'm in the company of a famous and wealthy celebrity athlete?"

He sighed and asked, "What do you want?"

"Beef, not dipped, with green peppers and red sauce. Fries and a Dr Pepper. If you want mozzarella sticks, we can share."

"That means you want most of them."

"Maybe you're smarter than I give you credit for, Mr. McKay." She headed down the hall to the restroom.

"Are you going to finish your sandwich?" he asked thirty minutes later. "If not, I'll finish it. I don't want to take it in the Jeep."

She rubbed her stomach. "I won't be able to eat another bite for days. Unless you want to grab a couple slices of chocolate cake. We could take them home. I'll even buy." She reached into her purse and pulled out two dollars.

"That will buy mine," he said.

She made a face and handed him a ten. "I want change back."

"No way. This won't cover your share of the gas."

"Are you going to make your baby sister pay for gas?"

"You aren't my sister, Cara."

She giggled and said, "Claire Halston thinks we are. I saw the look on her face when you explained how we grew up."

"You're exaggerating."

Caralyn shrugged. "Don't leave without me, or I'll eat both slices of cake."

"Wouldn't think of it."

She grabbed his keys. "Yes, you would."

"There are three cars in the driveway, Tuck. Park next door," Caralyn said two and a half hours later.

They pulled into the driveway at Grandma's house. Caralyn jumped out and hollered, "Will you grab my bags and take them inside, please? I need to see Mom and Dad."

"What makes you think they want to see you anymore than me?" he asked opening the back.

"Because they love me more than you, silly." She ran across the yard, jumped onto the porch, opened the wooden screen door and stepped inside to a crowded living room.

"Hello, Caralyn. We didn't expect you home this early," Mom said.

"Hi, we left a little earlier than planned, I guess," Caralyn replied trying to identify the ladies in the room. *Why are they all wearing red hats?*

"We are almost finished," Mom said.

"Where's Daddy?"

"He and Uncle Carlton are at the farm. Your grandfather needed help with the large door on the corn crib."

"I'll go outside and help Tucker with the luggage." She dashed outside as Tucker stepped onto Grandma Florence's porch. "Don't go in. I mean don't go in your house."

He set the luggage down. "Why not?"

She glanced over her shoulder. "It's weird."

"What's weird?"

"The living room was full of old ladies. That's what."

"So. Maybe they're friends of Mom."

She shook her head. "They were all wearing these old-fashioned red hats. It was spooky."

Tucker laughed and said, "Those are the ladies from the local Red Hat Society. Aunt Mary joined, and they are trying to convince Mom to become a member."

"Never heard of them. What do they do?"

"Social stuff," he said with a shrug. "I don't know exactly." He grinned and said, "Maybe you should join."

"Not a chance."

Tucker asked about his father and Caralyn explained.

"There's nothing in that old corn crib. Do you remember how we used to climb the ladder and play up there?"

"Yeah, and I remember seeing a rat once. I didn't know what it was at first. I was going to pet it."

"I wouldn't have let you get close. Sometimes they have rabies."

They went inside, and Caralyn looked around. "I should dust this weekend."

He wiped a finger on one of the end tables. "Guess so."

"Do you know if Derren and Natalie are coming into town?"

He shook his head. "They aren't. She made reservations in Branson to see some show. Derren was pissed, but she paid a lot of money for the show and a hotel."

She put a finger to her mouth.

"What?"

"I'm trying to remember what Derren looks like? Is he the one who's kinda short with red hair and a bit of a pot belly?"

"You must be thinking of Santa Claus," he teased. "Yeah, I miss him, too."

"Do you think he knew she would be so controlling? She wasn't like this before they got married."

"She was, but not to this degree." Tucker looked out the window. "Cara, look. The red hats are leaving. Do you think Mom's all right? They might have brainwashed her."

"You're a twerp. Let's talk to her."

They walked outside and saw Mom on the porch.

"Why were those old ladies here?" Caralyn asked.

"I invited them."

"Why?"

"They like to socialize. Most of them... some of them are widows and need to interact with like-minded women. Are you hungry?"

"We ate in New Lebanon," Tucker answered. "Do you think Dad needs any help?"

Mom shook her head. "He called a few minutes ago. He's on his way home. They fixed the door."

"I promised Mrs. Young I would eat dinner with them tonight. She said she needed to tell me something."

"It's all right," Mom said.

Tucker hesitated then asked, "Cara, would you like to watch the fireworks in Butler tonight?"

"Sure. I think Davey and Melissa are going."

Tucker drove to the Young house and saw a Realtor sign in the yard.

Mr. Young let him in and said, "You saw the sign, huh?"

"I did. Are you really selling it?"

"Mrs. Young wants to be closer to Sandy and the baby. We found jobs, and the cost of living is a lot less."

"I'll be sorry to see you go, but I understand. Don't tell anyone yet, but I'm thinking of moving, too."

"Out of Chicago?" he asked.

Tucker shook his head. "Probably still in the city, but maybe a suburb. The memories are getting to me. I need a new start."

"I understand, and won't even tell the wife."

"Thanks."

Tucker ate dinner and talked to his former in-laws until he needed to pick up Caralyn.

"Thanks for coming over," Mrs. Young said. "Have fun tonight."

Mr. Young winked at Tucker and shook his hand.

"Where should we sit?" Caralyn asked as they entered the football field in Butler.

"Anywhere you want. Maybe at the top."

She led him to the top row. Later she saw Davey and Melissa and stood to wave.

Davey spotted her and they joined them.

"I thought maybe you decided to watch from home," Caralyn said as Davey scooted past her.

"We can hear them and see some stuff, but not everything."

After the fireworks show Caralyn asked, "Can we stop at the Salty Dogs?"

"They have the best root beer," Melissa said.

Caralyn added, "I love their fries."

"Sure," Tucker said knowing he would have to pay. "Did I mention Nancy's parents are moving to Missouri?"

"No! Are they really?" Caralyn asked.

"There's a sale sign in the yard. They want to be closer to Sandy and Lloyd. I can't say I blame them."

"I can understand why."

He looked at Caralyn and wondered if he should reveal his thoughts about moving. He decided to wait.

"Do you want to go to church, Cara?" Tucker asked in the morning.

She checked the time and almost dropped the phone. "Would you mind if I stay home. We stayed out later than I expected."

"It's all right. You and Davey were having fun. A little too much fun according to the frown on Melissa's face."

"He's afraid to let Melissa do anything now that she's expecting."

"What?"

"Ooops! I wasn't supposed to say anything. They haven't told anyone yet."

"I won't spoil the surprise. Uncle Carlton will be thrilled especially if they have a girl."

Tucker went to church alone and decided to stop at the cemetery afterward. He parked the Jeep, walked to Nancy's site and looked around.

"Sorry, Nancy, but I feel funny talking to you in front of people. I need to tell you I've decided to move. I know you loved the apartment, and Caralyn will be mad, but I see you everywhere I look. I have to move if I want to get on with my life." He leaned over and pulled a weed. "I know you told me not to grieve too long, and get on with my life, but I'm not ready. I rarely see anyone other than the people at church, Caralyn and the guys I train with. I talk to Alphonse about God, and I've made a commitment like you did. At first I thought it was something I needed to do if I ever wanted to see you in heaven, but now I'm starting to understand I need a personal relationship with Jesus regardless of how you believed. Cara and I have gone to this church..."

He spent five minutes talking to her before he saw someone pull into the cemetery.

He stood up and said, "I'll see you later." He blew her a kiss and walked back to the Jeep. He realized it was the Young's car and decided to leave without talking to them.

"Are you ready to head home?" he asked Caralyn around three.

"Why so early? Have you got somewhere to be?"

"I need to get stuff done." He hugged his mother. "Sorry, for the quick visit, and I might not get back for a while."

"It's good to see you anytime you can make it home," she said.

"What about me?" Caralyn asked with a grin.

"I'm always happy to see my little girl," Dad said.

Caralyn smirked at Tucker and whispered, "Daddy loves me more."

Tucker shook his head and rolled his eyes.

Tucker pulled into the garage and carried Caralyn's bags to her apartment.

She found her keys in her purse and unlocked the door. "You were rather quiet coming home."

"Sorry. I wasn't much fun this weekend. I have a lot on my mind." He set the bags in her bedroom. "They were heavier coming home."

"More clothes. I understand. It will take time to get over Nancy."

He hugged her and headed upstairs. He booted up his computer and emailed his real estate agent.

"I'm ready to start looking," he whispered as he typed.

Chapter Nine

"Trent, I haven't heard from you in three months, one week and four days, but who's counting," Caralyn said as she giggled. "Why the surprise call?"

"I sent you an email two weeks ago, Cara."

"You did, but you didn't say much."

"I'm flying into the city for business Thursday morning and wondered if you were busy. Are you?"

"What time?"

"Nine."

"Let me check." She rustled some junk mail on the desk. "Oh, I'm sorry. I have to help the neighbors learn French."

"At least you used an original excuse," he replied. "I suppose I can take a train into the city and stay at one of those expensive hotels and not have to see you."

"Would you really come to Chicago and not see me?" She sat on the edge of the desk.

"Maybe, and it's a quick trip."

"Fine. I'll pick you up. You can stay with me if you want," she said without thinking how he might take her invitation. "How long will you be in town?"

"I fly out Saturday afternoon."

"That will give us a little time to catch up on stuff. I want to know everything about your social life."

He laughed and said, "I don't have a social life. My father was asking about you the other day."

"What did you tell him? How's he doing?"

"My mother gets on his case for working too many hours, but otherwise, he's okay."

"How was Alaska, or are you still living there?"

"I'm home now. I thought about getting my own place, but then I would have to pay rent and do my own cooking."

"You are so lazy and spoiled." She scooted off the desk. "I'll see you Thursday. Email or text me when you take off."

Wednesday Caralyn ran upstairs and told Tucker Trent was coming to town.

"Where is he staying?" Tucker asked as he loaded the washing machine and added too much soap. "At a hotel, I hope."

"I told him he could crash with me."

"Why? He was your boyfriend. Won't he want to try to get back together?" Tucker closed the lid and turned it on. "Are you still interested in him? You were pretty serious at one time, and he was an all right guy."

"Compared to Jeremiah, you mean. We were serious, but it didn't work out, and not only because I wouldn't move to Oregon. There were other issues I never mentioned to you."

He stared at her, but she didn't elaborate.

"I have an extra room." He pointed in that direction. "He could crash with me."

"As do I," she said smacking his arm. "I'm not going to jump in bed with him just because we have a history."

"If I remember right, he's pretty charming."

"Drop it, Tucker. I didn't have to tell you he was coming. I'm old enough to make my own decisions."

"Whatever." Tucker walked into his bedroom with the empty laundry basket and closed the door.

She stomped her foot and hollered, "You can be so infuriating at times, Tucker McKay."

"Ms. Dawson, it's so good to see you again. I had almost forgotten what you look like."

She laughed and responded, "It's a pleasure to see you again, Mr. Cussler. You are Trent Cussler, right? My memory of you has faded."

"Would a kiss spark your memory?"

"It might, but we don't want to cause a fire in Chicago."

They talked about family while walking to her car. She fought the heavy traffic and finally made it home. She pulled into the garage and took him upstairs.

"This is it."

Trent looked at the ceiling.

"Tucker lives above me, but he can't hear anything going on here."

"Good to know." He looked around the apartment. "This has more character than your apartment in New Lebanon."

"It's an older building, but solid as a mountain."

"The last time I visited you, I expected to stay in the spare bedroom."

"Which is where you *will* be sleeping this time. For sure."

"Just checking," he said with a grin. "I do need to take a cab downtown. I have a one o'clock meeting."

"Should I make dinner, or will you be home late, sweetheart?" she teased.

He held her close and could smell her shampoo. "All I need when I get home is to kiss my sweet loving wife."

"Just one kiss?"

He shook his head. "I know you're teasing."

He returned by nine.

"I'm sorry for working so late, Cara, but I am free all day tomorrow. We got everything done today."

"Good. Did you eat? I made spaghetti for myself."

"We ate at some fancy restaurant, but I bet your spaghetti was better."

"You're just saying that to flatter me."

"Is it working?" he asked taking off his suit coat and tie.

"You're still sleeping in the spare room. Do I need to lock my door, or will you promise not to wake me in the middle of the night?"

He grinned and said, "No promises."

"I'm locking my door. I remember what happened the last time."

"Do you have any requests for breakfast?" Caralyn asked.

Trent walked up behind her and put his arms around her waist. "Whatever you want is fine with me. How did you sleep?"

"Like a baby. Are you disappointed I made you stay in the spare room?"

"Yes and no. I didn't expect you to let me pick up where we left off in Oregon."

She turned around, put her hands around his neck and pressed into him. "I thought about it, but as much as I enjoyed our... you know... I couldn't do it again."

He kissed her cheek. "It's okay. We can have fun with our clothes on."

"You are so naughty. Sit down, and I'll make you a couple slices of burnt toast."

"Sounds heavenly," he teased.

"What would you like to see today?" she asked. "I have a few suggestions, but it's up to you."

"I've been to Chicago several times in the last ten years. I've seen most of the sights, but I want to know about your neighborhood. Take me on a tour of Holland Park."

"I can do that. I'll take you grocery shopping at the little store on the corner, and I can show you the campus of McCormick University."

"Let's eat lunch at your favorite local place," he said.

They left her apartment an hour later and didn't return until after eight.

"That was a full day, Caralyn. Did you keep me going so we wouldn't come back here and be bored and maybe find a way to..."

"No. You wanted to get to know my neighborhood and now you do."

"I didn't expect to meet Mrs. Campanella and hear her life story," he said with a laugh.

"She can talk your ear off, but she gets lonely now."

"It can't be easy for a cop's widow. He was so close to retiring, too."

"I try to stop by her shop once a week and buy something even if I don't need it."

72

He looked at the candles lined up on a shelf. "I'm sure she appreciates your business."

"Are you hungry? I have ice cream and half of an apple pie."

"Sounds good. Do you have any coffee?"

She checked the cabinet. "I do, but only decaf. I've been drinking it lately."

"I shouldn't drink caffeine at night, but I do at home. I'll try the fake coffee."

"Is there a clean towel in your bathroom, or do you need another one?" she asked a couple hours later.

"I can use the same one. It's still clean."

"I'll see you in the morning."

"Thanks for the tour, Cara. I had more fun than going to a museum," he said with a grin.

"Did Trent leave?" Tucker asked when Caralyn walked into his apartment Saturday afternoon.

"I took him to the airport this morning, and before you even ask, he slept in the spare room." She sat on a barstool and put her elbows on the counter. "I would be lying if I said I wasn't tempted to let him share my bed, but I managed to fight off my lustful thoughts."

"I wasn't going to ask, Cara."

"That's why I'm telling you. You are a true gentleman."

"And a scholar?"

She didn't lift her head and answered, "Don't push your luck. What are your plans for tonight? I know you worked out this morning."

"I'm supposed to meet with a guy later to check out some properties."

"Are you going to invest some of your salary? You could probably buy this building, and then I wouldn't have to pay rent." She got up and moved to the couch. "Maybe I should buy a house or something. My trust is growing, and Beth said I should use some of it."

He joined her on the couch and she moved her feet to his lap. He rubbed them without her asking.

"We could buy a building together, or maybe a house in Stockton Woods."

"Why? You and Beth already own Grandma's house."

"I meant a different house. Never mind." She closed her eyes and sighed. "That feels good. Did Nancy let you massage her feet?"

He stood up and walked away.

"Tuck, I'm sorry. I didn't mean it like that."

He waved but wouldn't turn around. She walked up behind him and put her arms around his waist.

"Please don't be mad at me," she whispered.

He did an about-face and lifted her chin. "I'm not upset with you. I'm mad at myself."

"Why?"

"Let's sit on the couch. I need to tell you something."

She sat at one end with her feet under her. He sat with his hands on his knees and stared at the floor.

"Tell me, Tuck."

He looked at her. "I'm going to move."

She tilted her head. "Did you get traded? It's okay. I can move to wherever you're living after I finish my degree."

"No, Carrie. I didn't get traded or cut. I can't live here anymore because of the memories. Everything in this apartment reminds me of her."

"We could switch," she offered.

He shook his head. "Wouldn't matter. My agent is looking for a place closer to the United Center. Maybe in the suburbs. Not sure where I'll end up, but I can't stay here." He looked at her and saw a tear escape. "I'm sorry, Carrie. I know you love living here. You can stay. Just because I'm moving doesn't mean you have to."

"Part of why I love this place is knowing you're right above me. It won't be the same if you leave."

"I have to, but it won't be right away. I want to find somewhere nicer. Maybe more modern."

"But this place is built like a bank vault. It would survive an earthquake," she said.

"Yes, but my heart won't."

Caralyn waited while Tucker talked to Pastor Aaron after church the next day.

"I read the chapter earlier this week, but I didn't think of the point you made," Tucker said.

Pastor Aaron smiled and explained, "I wouldn't have interpreted it that way, but I read a book by Joseph Hoople and he brought out the point I used today."

"You've said previously how you can read a passage again and get a whole new meaning from it. I haven't read the Bible all the way through, so it's all new to me."

Claire walked up to Caralyn and asked, "How have you been. We missed you last week."

"Tuck and I went home for the Fourth. How are you? I loved the song you sang at the end."

"Thank you."

"I think I've heard it on the radio. Is it a popular song?" Caralyn asked.

"It is," Claire said with a smile. "It's from Emmy Colasanti's latest CD. Have you heard of her?"

"Tucker told me she's married to the singer in Fridays At Five."

"She did a concert here a couple years ago. She has an amazing voice," Claire said. "What do you do to keep busy during the week? Do you have a job?"

Caralyn looked at Tucker. *Are you going to keep asking questions about his sermon? You took a lot of notes.* She switched her attention to Claire. "I don't have a real job. I'm working on my master's degree at McCormick University. I'll be finished by the end of the summer."

"Maybe we can get together during the week sometime. I am usually home by four. My school gets out at three, but I have to stay until three thirty."

75

"I could try to find the time. This week an old friend flew into the city for a business meeting. I picked him up, and he stayed with me. I didn't want him to waste money on a hotel."

"He must be a close friend."

"He lived across the hall from me at MCU. We dated for a while, but our relationship ended because he wanted me to move to Oregon to live with him."

"Oh," Claire said. She cleared her throat and said, "He must have been disappointed."

"His father was more disappointed," she said with a grin. "We decided to just be friends, and that's all we are," Caralyn said after seeing the look in Claire's eyes.

"I didn't mean to upset you, Caralyn. I shouldn't have assumed anything. Forgive me?"

"No harm done."

Chapter Ten

"No, Caralyn, I am not changing my mind," Tucker said. "I found a better place for me, and I've already signed the lease. It's a done deal."

She plopped onto his couch, crossed her arms over her chest and stuck out her bottom lip. "You don't care about me. You are only thinking about yourself."

"I do care about you. You're being a baby."

He walked past her. She stuck out a foot to trip him, but he avoided it.

"No, you don't. You wouldn't leave me here all alone if you did." She jumped up and followed him into his bedroom. "You've cleared out most of Nancy's things. How does the apartment still remind you of her?"

He stared mutely at her.

She waved a hand dismissively. "Dumb question. Sorry."

He opened his closet door, looked inside then turned to Caralyn. "How many boxes do I need to pack this stuff? I'm taking it with me."

She stood next to him and looked. "Four or five large ones. More if they're smaller." She moved and sat on the edge of his bed. "How many bedrooms does your new place have?"

"Three. Why?" He turned to look at her and shook his head. "No way, Cara."

She plopped onto her back. "I wasn't going to ask if I could move in."

"Don't lie to me." He sat next to her. "Why is this so hard for you? We've been apart before. You were in France for a whole semester."

"That's different."

He laughed, and she smacked him with a pillow.

"It's not funny."

"I'm still in the city. It's not like I'm moving to Cleveland or Phoenix or..."

"You might end up in one of those places eventually."

"Don't you know any guys at school you'd like to date?" he asked. "And I don't mean any John Smiths."

"No."

"Come on. There has to be a few guys."

She sat up and answered, "There are plenty of guys. I see hundreds of them every day I have a class. Maybe not hundreds, but I see bunches. There are even a few I consider interesting and might want to get to know better."

"When was the last time you went on a date?" He stood up and pulled her up, too. "A real date with the possibility of romance." He shook a finger at her. "I didn't say sex. Romance. It's different."

"I know the difference."

"So, when was it? Your last real date."

"It was in 2002, I believe."

"You were thirteen. I'm asking a serious question."

"I haven't had a *boyfriend* since Trent. I've gone out with groups quite often, but not any solo dates. When are you going to think about dating again?"

"Are you nuts? Nancy's only been gone since June. It will take me years before I even think about another woman."

She grinned and said, "You'll get horny..."

"Don't go there."

"One of my professors is single."

"How old is he?"

"In his sixties," she answered with a giggle.

"Real cute."

She walked into the living room and sat on the couch again. "I could email Mr. Green, and see if I should drive down to Fremont for a visit."

"To what end?" He walked into the kitchen and leaned on the counter. "He's like fifteen years older than you and probably remarried by now."

"Maybe not. We probably would have heard if he did."

"You should think about someone closer to your age."

"What about someone between your age and Mr. Green?"

He opened the fridge and inspected the contents. "You don't need my permission to date someone. You're twenty-one and legal. Do you need any mustard or mayonnaise? I'm not taking it with me."

"I'll use it. How much is it going to cost for the movers?"

"Too much, but I can't do it myself. It's not like college. I've got more stuff."

Tuesday evening Caralyn went out for pizza with the regular group of eight from her class. She sat next to Te'von Beltran because there was an empty chair.

"Hello, Caralyn. Did you understand the point Dr. Summerall was trying to make at the end of his lecture?"

"I understood it, but I don't necessarily agree. I thought he was joking at first," she answered.

Their waitress walked up with an order pad to take drink orders.

"You're old enough to legally drink now, right?" Te'von asked.

"I am, but I'll stick to Dr Pepper."

"That's okay. I'll split a pitcher with you. I'm not pressuring you into anything."

The college-age waitress took their orders with a half-smile and walked away.

Te'von watched her then turned his attention back to Caralyn. "Did your friend move out?"

She shook her head. "Not yet, but he will be gone before the end of the month."

"He was married to one of your close friends, right?" Te'von asked.

"Yes, but she passed away. I told you, right?"

"You did, but you're pretty reserved about your private life."

"I don't mean to be mysterious, but I don't talk about myself a lot." *I've never told you Tucker's name, or anything about growing up together. I've certainly never talked about my love life.*

They listened to the conversation at the table until the waitress returned with their drinks. Te'von poured the Dr. Pepper for Caralyn.

"Thank you. You usually drink beer. You don't have to drink the pop. Marlene doesn't drink beer. We usually share a pitcher."

"I don't mind sharing with you."

The pizzas arrived during a lull in the conversation. Caralyn grabbed two slices of cheese pizza and looked at Te'von.

He filled his plate with pizza and whispered, "You are rather introverted."

"Not always, but most of the time."

An hour later as the group was dispersing, Te'von asked, "Can I talk to you a second?"

"Okay."

"Would you be interested in seeing a show, or having dinner with me this weekend?"

"Okay, but do I have to choose?"

He laughed and said, "We could do both or something else. One of my friends plays soccer in a league."

"We could wait to decide." She smiled at him.

"Did you have any trouble finding my building?" Caralyn asked early Saturday afternoon when Te'von met her outside.

"Your directions were spot on. Are you sure you don't mind walking? I could spring for a cab, or we could ride the bus? I don't own a car. Too expensive in the city."

"I like to walk."

He smiled at her. "I've never mentioned it, but I think you're the prettiest girl in class."

She grinned and replied, "Thank you, but there are only six women, and the others are much older."

"Let me rephrase. You are the prettiest girl in school."

"That's better, but it's not accurate," she said as they waited at the corner for traffic. "Where is your friend's soccer game?"

He told her.

"That's close to where we have our class."

"That's why I thought we could walk."

The game was underway when they got to the park.

"We can sit on the incline if you don't mind," he said leading the way.

She followed and they watched Te'von's friend play.

"I get worn out watching them run," he said. "You mentioned playing sports in high school."

"I was a female jock. I played softball, basketball, and volleyball. Plus, I was a cheerleader for the boys' basketball team."

"When did you have time to study?"

"I made time. I don't mean to brag, but I was the class valedictorian."

"Pretty and smart. A great combination."

She poked his arm. "You're not so shabby, Te'von. Where did you grow up?"

"Brooklyn Heights, New York. I have five older sisters. I'm the only brother."

He talked about his family for a time because she kept asking questions.

"Are you ever going to talk about your family?" he finally asked.

"My parents were killed in a car accident when I was a baby. I was raised by my grandmother."

"I'm so sorry, Caralyn."

Should I mention the rest? She gazed at him. *I'll save it for later. He doesn't need to know everything right away.*

"My father left home when I was three. Maybe four. I rarely see or hear from him. My mama raised us. We all have college educations. I'm the last one to finish. My oldest sister is a school superintendent in Virginia..."

She listened as he told her what each sister did for a living.

"Are you hungry?" she asked.

"All this talking has whetted my appetite. Where would you like to go?"

81

"Do you like Mexican? If so, I know great place."
She took him to Tito's Casa.

"We don't need to go to a show," she said after they left Tito's. "It's a beautiful day. Let's walk around the neighborhood."

"Sounds okay. I'd rather talk to you than sit in a theater to watch a movie." He took her hand, and they walked back to the park by the university.

"We could sit on the bench and watch birds or dogs chasing squirrels."

She giggled and sat. "Do the dogs ever win?"

"Doubtful," he said. He leaned close and kissed her tenderly.

A few minutes later she said, "We haven't bothered looking for birds, squirrels or any animals."

"Should I stop kissing you?"

"I doubt if there are any animals around. If we want to see them, we could go to the zoo."

"Are you busy tomorrow?"

"I don't have any plans."

"I could pick you up around noon."

"Okay, but I'll drive since you don't have a car."

"Deal."

"Are you coming to church with me?" Tucker asked Sunday morning.

"Sorry, but I can't."

"Why not?"

"Because I have plans," she answered without elaborating.

He stared at his phone for a second. "Do you have a date?"

"Well, you told me I should go out again. I went on a date yesterday, and today we're going to the zoo."

"That's okay, but I think I should meet this man before you go out again," he said with a grin.

"Are you trying to be Daddy?"

"Is it working?"

82

"No! I'm not letting you meet him unless he proposes," she teased.

He laughed and said, "It's my own fault. I told you to start seeing people other than Trent. Can you tell me his name?"

"It's Te'von Beltran, and I've known him for almost a year. He's one of the guys in our group that goes out after class."

"I've never known anyone with that name," Tucker said.

"I knew it would pique your interest. He comes from a mixed racial marriage. His father was African American and his mother is Puerto Rican. His father left years ago." She told Tucker more about Te'von.

"He sounds all right."

Caralyn laughed. "I'm so glad he meets with your approval, *Daddy*."

"Just make sure you're home by eight o'clock. Tomorrow is a school day, young lady."

"I feel weird letting you drive," Te'von said on their way to the Jefferson Park Zoo. He patted her knee. "But it gives me a chance to look at your legs without you noticing."

"You saw my legs yesterday," she said zipping through a yellow light.

"Today I'm going to pay closer attention, though."

She looked at his legs. "Why aren't you wearing shorts? Are you afraid of getting sunburned?"

He laughed. "It would take a lot for me to get burned."

She parked, and he paid the entrance fee.

"What would you like to see first?"

"The snakes," she said.

He jumped back. "Really?"

She giggled and took his hand. "No, but they don't scare me. I want to see the monkeys, elephants, and giraffes, for sure."

After four hours at the zoo, they headed back to Holland Park.

"Would you like to come upstairs?" she asked after parking in the garage.

"Is my other option to stay in the garage?"

She laughed and said, "You could stay in the alley, but it might get rather warm."

"Then I'd love to come upstairs."

She showed him the apartment, and they sat on the couch.

"You've got a nice place, Caralyn." He looked at the walls and furnishings. "You don't have to answer, but how can you afford it?"

"I'm Dr. Summerall's mistress. He pays the rent. All I have to do is sleep with him."

Te'von stared at her with an open mouth.

"How else could a girl my age afford it?"

He cleared his throat. "Does he mind you seeing other people?"

"He knows I have different needs than his. He doesn't mind as long as I'm discreet, and available when he needs me. It's not usually more often than once a week. He comes here and spends the night." She sat with her back against the couch's arm with her knees drawn to her chest and waited for a response.

He took a moment to process the information, shrugged and said, "I'm surprised. I thought you were possibly a virgin since you are rather young and shy." He stared at her legs. "This changes how I look at you."

"Literally," she said with a grin. "You're staring at my legs again."

He chuckled and looked away. "Sorry, but you do have nice legs, and... you know... the rest of you is pretty amazing, too. I can see why he likes you."

"I shocked you. I can tell it changes things."

He stood up and walked into the kitchen. He got a drink of water before he walked back to the couch. He looked at her and started to say something but stopped.

"You can tell me," she said.

He paced for a moment then stood before her. "I don't believe you. I can't figure out how you can afford to live here yet, but I know you aren't Dr. Summerall's mistress."

84

She grinned and asked, "What gave it away? I thought I was rather convincing. I almost believed it myself for a split-second."

"A couple things." He walked to the desk and picked up her open Bible. "I doubt if a mistress would be reading the Gospel of John." Then he walked up to a photograph on the wall. "Second, this is you with who I can only assume to be your adopted family. You are quite young in this photo..."

"I was fourteen."

"But I can tell it's you. A mistress wouldn't leave this photo up."

"Anything else, Mr. Sherlock Holmes?"

"You would need to be a highly skilled actress to pull off the innocence you exude."

"I'm not..."

He cut her off with a wave. "I'm not talking about any sexual experience you have. Your innocence comes from the heart." He did a quick about-face, walked back to the couch, sat closer to her and touched her knees. "In conclusion, I believe the only way you can afford the rent on this apartment is..."

"Yes, Mr. Holmes."

He shrugged and said, "I haven't the foggiest clue. No idea whatsoever."

She giggled and said, "Should I tell you, or will it be more fun to pretend I'm his mistress?"

He leaned closer and kissed her. "Tell me how your affair started, Ms. Dawson. I want to hear all the sordid details."

Chapter Eleven

"That's everything, Cara. All that's left in the apartment is my duffel bag," Tucker said.

"Did you double-check each room? The movers might have missed something in a closet or a cabinet," she said as she walked into his bedroom.

Tucker watched as she looked into the closet. "Caralyn, the movers are ready to leave. I have to give my keys to the super."

"Why can't I go with you to your new place? I can do something to help."

"It will be chaos today. You can come over tomorrow night. We can order a pizza, or whatever. You can bring Te'von if you want."

"Are you going to church in the morning?" she asked. "You could pick me up, and I'll go with."

"Sorry, but I told Pastor Aaron I wouldn't be there because of the move. He offered to bring some guys over and help, but I told him I was already paying the movers to do it."

She wandered into the kitchen and boosted herself onto the countertop. "What will I do if my new neighbors are jerks? They could be drug dealers, or the landlord could rent the unit to Russian spies or gangsters."

"It won't matter, Cara. The floor is soundproof. They could set off a bomb upstairs, and you wouldn't hear it." He grinned and said, "Russian gangsters, huh?"

She made a face at him. "You're teasing me, and I'm about to cry."

He walked up to her and held her. She put her head on his shoulders and cried softly.

She straightened up after a moment, took a deep breath and sighed. "Okay, I'm through feeling sorry for myself." She hopped down, took his hand and led him out of the apartment. "The super's waiting. The landlord better not try to raise my rent."

"Didn't you sign a new lease?" Tucker asked as they passed her floor. "Your old one was only for a year."

She shook her head and bounced down the stairs with more life. "With everything going on, I haven't signed a new one. He told me I could wait until September when school starts to sign one."

"But you'll be finished with school before then, right?" he asked as he opened the entrance door.

"Yes, I will have my master's degree by the end of the month."

He tossed his envelope with the keys and garage remote to the super and looked at her. "I can tell by the way you're chewing your lip you've got a plan. Spill it. You aren't moving in with me."

"I've been looking for a job in the city, but no one in the publishing industry wants to hire me except as a secretary. The only other offers I've had are to be a translator. I could do it, but it's not where my heart lies."

"What are you going to do? You could keep going to school and get a doctorate. You're only eighteen..."

"You know how old I am, *Daddy*. Stop teasing me."

"You don't even need a job. You could live off the interest of your trust."

"Beth has a job. She's living off the money she and Ray earn. I want to be self-sufficient like them."

"And me?" he asked with a grin.

She swatted his arm. "You play basketball. That won't last forever, and you'll have to find a real job."

"I am planning for life after the NBA. I want to get into coaching. That's a job with a future."

"Sure, a future of getting fired if your team doesn't make the Final Four, or win the NBA title."

"A good coach will always be in demand." He saw her grin and shook his head. "I set myself up for that, huh?"

"Yes, but it's too easy to use."

"What are your plans?"

"It depends on whether I find the right job before the end of the year."

"And if you don't?"

"I have other options available. I could become the mistress of one of the hot professors."

"Did you try to sell that story to Te'von?"

"Yes, and he believed me at first. I had him going."

Tucker rubbed his jaw. "You know. It might not be a bad idea. You're still young and pretty enough..."

"Tucker James! I am not going to sleep with a man to get him to pay my rent," she said with a straight face. "He will have to help me get my novel published, too."

"You're goofy, Cara. I got to run. The movers are waiting."

"Call me tomorrow as soon as it's okay for me to visit."

"Maybe I want some alone time first."

"Be that way, twerp brain. I know the new address."

"Are you sure he won't mind you bringing me?" Te'von asked the next afternoon. "He might not want to let me see his place with boxes scattered everywhere."

Caralyn laughed and said, "Knowing Tuck like I do, I'd bet he's got everything unpacked, and his apartment will look like he's lived there for years."

"Not likely if he's anything like me," Te'von said. "I've still got boxes of stuff."

"When are you going to invite me over? I might want to see how messy you are."

"I admit it. I live like a slob. If you want to see the mess, we can stop there later."

"I'm used to guys living in squalor. Tucker, Derren and Richard shared a two-bedroom unit for three years. I spent more time cleaning it up than they did."

He stared at her mutely.

"What?"

"Was one of them your boyfriend?"

She blushed and said, "Of course not. I was Professor Harrison's mistress."

"That's your way of evading the question, Caralyn."

She touched his arm tenderly and said, "You're so smart."

Caralyn turned onto W. Warren Street. "His building is that one, but I have to find how to get to the alley. His garage is in back."

Eventually, she found the way through the maze of one-way streets and parked in the alley next to the garage.

Te'von got out and looked around. "This is closer to the United Center, but it's... you know."

"Yeah, this building isn't as nice, but he had to move because of the memories."

"Why doesn't he buy a house in the suburbs? I'm sure he could afford it," Te'von asked.

"He told me he doesn't want the hassle of owning one yet. He's talked about buying one in the area where we grew up."

They followed the sidewalk along the side of the four-story building to the front entrance. She pressed the button for his unit.

"He's already got his fake name up," she said.

"Fake name? What do you mean?"

She pointed to the list of tenants. "He uses the name Jim Stockton because he thinks it will fool anyone trying to find out where he lives."

"Why? They can't get in the building unless he buzzes them in."

She shrugged and pressed the button for 301.

"Come on up, Cara,"

She heard a click and pushed on the heavy door. They walked up the wide stairs to the third floor.

Tucker was waiting with his door open.

"How did you know it was me?" she asked. "This is Te'von Beltran. The guy I told you about."

"Security camera. But I let you in anyway." He shook hands with Te'von. "Come on in."

They looked around and Caralyn said, "What did I tell you?"

"What are you whispering about?" Tucker asked.

"I told Te'von you'd have everything unpacked." She walked around and even looked in a closet.

"I don't like to live out of boxes."

"Are you going to give us a tour?" she asked while looking into the kitchen.

He pointed and said, "The kitchen's in there. We're in the living room, and the bedrooms and bathrooms are over there."

"You're a big help." She checked the first bedroom as Te'von followed. "This is the master bedroom." She checked the second bedroom and looked at Tucker. "Is that a new bedroom set?"

"It's new to me, but I bought it from the previous tenants."

"This is my bedroom," she whispered to Te'von.

Tucker shook his head. "I heard that. You can visit occasionally, but you aren't moving in, Caralyn."

After inspecting all the rooms, Caralyn and Te'von joined Tucker on the couch. Tucker and Te'von talked about sports.

"I saw a photo in Caralyn's apartment of her at fourteen with her adopted family. That was you in the picture, right?" Te'von asked.

Tucker nodded and asked, "How much has she told you?"

Te'von told him the little background he knew.

"After her grandmother passed away, my parents became her guardian, but they never formally adopted her." He looked at Caralyn, grinned and said, "Thank the Lord for that. She'd be my sister..."

"You're a twerp," she said. "His parents are my parents, but not technically, if you get my meaning."

"I'm close to my sisters, but we are biological siblings." He told Tucker about his family.

"Can we order a pizza?" Caralyn asked. "I'm hungry."

"We can have one delivered, or go out. Which would you prefer, Te'von?" Tucker asked.

He shrugged and said, "Doesn't matter."

They ordered one and ate in the living room.

"Since you aren't going to let me move in, I suppose I should take Te'von home," Caralyn said around ten.

"Are you going home for Labor Day?" Tucker asked.

"Yes, are you?"

He shook his head. "I can't get away. I have a career that demands my time."

"This is my last week of classes. Actually, I only have two classes. I finished all the requirements for my master's."

"Are you going to start working on a PhD?"

"No, I'm still looking for a job. If I can't find anything interesting, I might finish my novel and try to get it published."

"Call me later this week. We can do something if you want." He looked at Te'von, who was waiting by the stairs. "Unless you're too busy."

"Are you busy Wednesday evening?" Te'von asked over the phone Monday.

"Not really," she answered.

"Would you like to do something? Dinner? Maybe a show?"

"Still too poor to afford both," she teased.

"If you insist," he said with a laugh.

"I have two interviews Wednesday, but no plans for the evening."

"Would seven work?"

"Are you coming here, or do I need to pick you up?"

"I can come to your place. If it's not raining, we could walk to Tito's Casa again."

"Okay. Call me before you head over."

"Is that so you can clean your apartment before I show up?" he asked with a chuckle.

"No, I might be worn out from the interviews," she replied.

"Are we still on for tonight?" Te'von asked

Caralyn looked at the clock. "I just got home. Would you mind if I ask for a rain check?"

"You can't be too tired to eat. We could order something. Pizza, or the Chinese place looked good."

She sighed and said, "I might not be very good company."

"Seeing you will be enough for me."

He arrived shortly after seven with Chinese carryout.

"I took the liberty of ordering for us." He set the three bags on the counter. "Three different entrees, so you should like one of them."

"I'll get the plates."

"How was your interview? Interviews, I mean. Did they hire you on the spot?" He pulled the containers out and opened them. "Orange chicken. Sweet and sour pork." He opened the last one. "Chicken chop suey as a safety entree in case you didn't like the others."

They sat at the counter to eat.

"Do you like egg rolls?" he asked.

"Not really," she answered scooping fried rice onto her plate. "Which one do you like best?"

He pointed to the orange chicken. "I'll share though."

"You can have the chop suey if you'll eat it," he offered later. "We didn't touch it. I'll know better next time."

She put it in the fridge. "You can take the orange chicken and sweet and sour pork. There's not a lot left."

He put those containers next to the chop suey.

She tossed the egg rolls in the trash.

"What should we do now?" He made himself comfortable on the couch.

She stood in front of him. "I'm really bushed. Would you mind if we call it an early night?"

"From your tone, I think you're trying to tell me something, right?"

"No, I'm just tired. Maybe we can do something this weekend."

"Friday work for you?"

"Saturday would be better," she answered.

He grinned and asked, "Is Friday your night with Dr. Summerall?"

"Yeah, I have to pay the rent somehow."

"It's a perfect afternoon for a soccer game," Te'von said as they left Caralyn's apartment. He waited on the steps as she talked to one of the neighbors. She said goodbye and Te'von took her in his arms and kissed her.

"What was that for?" she asked.

"Can't I kiss a pretty girl if I want?"

"Maybe. Do you meet lots of pretty girls and kiss them without asking?" She walked down the steps to the street as he followed.

"Hundreds," he teased.

She looked over her shoulder and said, "Maybe you should find one of them to watch the game."

"I'd rather be with you." He caught up to her, put an arm around her shoulders and kissed her cheek.

She moved his hand away. "Don't, Te'von." *Am I going to have to fight you off all day? I'm not in the mood and don't think I have the energy.*

"My schedule for next semester is heavier than I anticipated."

They crossed the side street and she said, "I thought you only needed six hours to finish your degree."

"Yes, but I want to get another degree..."

She listened to him with one ear as she walked. *When I first moved here, I thought it was the perfect neighborhood.* She glanced down and noticed two broken syringes and a pile of cigarettes butts at the corner of the apartment building. *Did I always overlook stuff like this, or is the area getting worse?*

"... I will probably move back to Brooklyn Heights to help take care of my mama, but eventually I want to settle in upper New York."

Caralyn heard him mention Brooklyn Heights. *I have visited Richard, and I could see myself living in Manhattan, but not anywhere else in the city.* She stubbed her toe on a broken section of sidewalk. *Who am I kidding? Now that I've finished school, I want to go home. I'm not like Beth. I don't need the social life the way she does...*

"Where are you?" Te'von asked. "I asked if you want something to drink."

"Sorry, my mind was wandering. I'm good for now."

"Let me know if you change your mind. I'll buy the tasty beverages.".

He continued to talk more than normal.

Has he always been this garrulous, and I tuned it out, or is today an exception?

He took her hand in his and they found a place to sit on the incline to watch the game.

"Why do you like soccer so much?" she asked after the game. "There were only two goals the entire game, and maybe a total of ten attempts. Most of the time the action was in the center of the field. One team would take the ball away, and the other would take it right back. I'd rather watch football or basketball."

"We played soccer where I grew up because it was easier. All we needed was a ball and the street."

"Would you watch if your friend wasn't playing?"

"I would still enjoy watching." He took her hand, pulled her close and kissed her.

She backed away after the kiss.

"What's wrong? You don't seem to be yourself today."

"It's nothing. Can we head back to my place, please?"

He smiled, kissed her again and said, "That's more like it."

"Stop it, Te'von! That's not what I see happening." She backed away, turned and started walking.

"I know a club you would like. We can have dinner, go dancing and then it might be too late for me to catch a bus home. I could crash at your place. I don't have a class until ten, and you don't have to go to work or a class. It will be the perfect time to..."

She stopped and pushed him in the chest. "No! I don't want to go out tonight, and you are not spending the night. In fact, you should catch a bus home now."

"I don't want to go home. I want to spend the day with you, girl."

"Don't *girl* me, Te'von." She walked away with her heart racing.

He waited for her to stop and turn around, but she didn't. "Caralyn, don't walk away mad."

"I am upset because you are assuming too much about our relationship."

He raced after her. "We are going to get there at some point. Why not tonight?"

"You are presuming too much." She pointed and said, "If you hurry, you can catch that bus."

He clenched his jaw and made a fist. "I don't want to catch a bus."

She noticed his hand and held her breath. *You wouldn't dare.*

He realized he was close to letting his anger get the best of him. He relaxed his hand and said, "I'm sorry. We have known each other for over a year. You know me well enough to be more than friends. I don't want to waste any more time playing dating games."

"Neither do I." She sighed and said, "I'm sorry. If this was another day, I might be willing to let you stay, but not today."

He looked at her for a moment. Then a smile slowly appeared. "I grew up with older sisters, remember? I understand about certain times."

She rolled her eyes. "It's not that. Why do men always assume it's that time of the month if a girl doesn't jump into bed with them?"

He shrugged.

She stomped her foot and marched away.

"Is this still because of your friend passing away?" he asked. "I'm sorry about that, and I want to help you any way I can."

"I'm not sure there's anything you can do. It will take time." She stopped walking and faced him. "Exactly what kind of help were you thinking of offering?"

"I thought being together at night might help."

She shook her head. "No way I am going to sleep with you to try and forget Nancy."

"I could spend the night and you could tell me everything about her or your friend Tucker."

"I don't think so, Te'von. I'll talk to you later." She walked away.

"Call me if you change your mind. Even if all you want is to talk."

"Goodbye, Te'von," she said without looking back. *How stupid do you think I am? You wouldn't be satisfied with talking. I learned my lesson with Jeremiah.*

He watched her for a moment before turning around and heading to the bus stop.

Chapter Twelve

"I'm on my way to Stockton Woods, Te'von. What's on your mind?"

"I want to apologize..."

She checked for traffic and made a right turn. "You've apologized three times this week."

"Are you still upset with me? I can't help how I feel about you. I want more than a *buddy* to go to the zoo, or watch a game with. I have other needs."

"I know you do, and I want that also, but our goals are nearly incompatible. Our relationship would be doomed to failure from the start. Trust me. I've been there."

"How can you say that? I don't understand. Give me an example."

"Okay. You want to move back to New York. I want to live in a small town here in the Midwest."

"You like the city."

"I have enjoyed living in the city while I was in school. I don't want to stay here unless I can find the perfect job."

"You are being unrealistic. No company is going to hire you to be the CEO," he joked.

"That's not my idea of a perfect job."

"I was teasing. You need to be patient. You will find a job. You are the smartest lady I know."

She chuckled and said, "Your sisters are smarter than me. Isn't one of them a surgeon?"

"Okay, you're one of the smartest women I know," he said then laughed. "Can we get together when you get home?"

"I'm going home, Te'von."

"I meant back to the city. You aren't moving this weekend, are you?"

She shook her head. "Don't be silly. I have too much stuff to fit in my car. I will text you when I get back."

"I'll be waiting."

She smiled and waved at someone she only knew by sight when she drove around the curve and entered Stockton Woods. She saw Dad McKay mowing the yard when she pulled into the driveway. He stopped the mower and walked toward her car.

She jumped out, smiled and said, "I should hire you to take care of my yard, too."

"I'm not sure you could afford me. I'm the most expensive landscaper in the county." He held out his arms. "I'm not too sweaty for a hug, am I?"

"Never."

Mom McKay stepped onto the front porch. "I didn't expect you this early." She looked in the car. "Are you alone?"

"Yes, Tucker is busy. You know that, Mom."

"Yes, but I thought you might be bringing someone with you."

"Mom! Te'von is only a friend, but I may have to break up with him."

"Why would you need to break up with a friend?" Mom asked with a grin.

"It's complicated. Can we talk about it after lunch?"

"Of course, sweetie," Dad said.

Caralyn and Sarah frowned at him.

He shrugged and said, "I should be allowed to know some things about my daughter and her *friends*."

"He has different goals for his life than I do," Caralyn said as she set the table for lunch.

"For example?" Mom asked.

"He wants to move back to New York City." She wiped some spots from a glass, then set it back in the sink and got another one from the cabinet. "There's no way I'm moving there. Richard says he likes living in the city, but his place is smaller than a closet. I don't want to spend a fortune to live somewhere unless I love it."

"Would you consider living in Paris?" Mom asked as she sliced a tomato. "You enjoyed living there."

"I did love it, but I don't want to live that far away from everyone."

"That's sweet. You would miss your family even though you are growing up."

"I would miss you guys, but I am not sure about Tucker."

Mom looked at her expecting to see a grin. "You look serious. Did something happen between you two?"

Caralyn opened the fridge and took out a bowl of homemade potato salad. "No, but he is still grieving and it has changed everything."

"He needs time, Cara."

"I understand, and I miss her, too. Not the same way as he does, but she was my closest friend. I'm entitled to grieve, too."

Dad walked into the kitchen, sat in his chair and said, "I'm glad that's finished. We seriously need to hire someone to do the mowing and landscaping. My poor back isn't up to the strain anymore."

"You can hire someone," Caralyn said. "I can pay them."

"Oh, did you get a job?" Dad asked.

"Not yet, but..."

"No buts. You aren't using your money to pay our bills. I appreciate the offer, but we will find a company willing to do it."

"Didn't you have someone mowing earlier this year?"

"A local kid, but he left for college." Dad shook his head. "Why would he want to spend all that money to go to college when he could have earned fifteen dollars every time he mowed our yards?"

Caralyn grinned and said, "If you are paying that much, I will take the job."

"What would you like to drink, Jim?" Mom asked. "I made sweet tea or you can have ice water."

"Sounds good to me." He looked at Caralyn and asked, "Where is your new friend? What happened between you?"

"We are incompatible as anything more than friends, and that's all you need to know." She kissed her father's forehead. "I'm glad I found out before we got too serious."

Dad looked at her.

"We didn't sleep together," Caralyn said.

Dad stood up and checked his hands. "I need to clean up before we eat."

Caralyn grinned and said, "All I have to do to embarrass him is mention sex."

"Mom, would you mind if I go to church this morning?" Caralyn asked.

"Not at all. I was going to ask if you would like to go. The church is looking for a new minister. The bishop doesn't have anyone to replace Rev. Grissom when he retires."

"They need a younger minister or else the church is going to wither and die. The last time I was there, I didn't see a single person my age."

"There are too many distractions for young people these days," Mom said. "If you wait, we will ride with you."

"I can wait." She heard her phone chirp and looked to see who had texted her. "It's Te'von. I should answer it."

"You could use your phone and talk to him like in the old days," Dad said with a grin.

Caralyn shook her head. "No one uses a phone to talk anymore. It just isn't done."

"Thank you for coming to see us," Mom said Sunday evening as Caralyn was getting ready to leave.

"I will make a decision this week about if I want to stay in Chicago or come home. The landlord keeps texting about a new lease. I'm leaning toward coming home. I can write a book anywhere."

"You take all the time you need to decide," Mom said.

"The house is there if you need to use it," Dad said. He kissed her cheek. "Drive safely."

"Oh, Daddy. You always spoil my fun. I was going to drive like a maniac, and see if I could outrun the law."

"How was your weekend?" Te'von asked Monday evening.

"It was good to see everyone. I had time to think about my future."

"That sounds ominous."

"I'm going to give up my apartment and move back to Stockton Woods. The city isn't where I want to spend the rest of my life."

Te'von didn't respond.

"Are you still there?"

"I'm here. I guess this is it for us, right?"

"I'm sorry, but that's the way it has to be."

"How big is Stockton Woods? How many people?"

She laughed and replied, "A few less than your typical block in Brooklyn Heights."

"That's a pity. Can we have dinner before you move out?"

"I will make dinner if you promise to behave."

"I don't make promises I have no intention of keeping," he said with a laugh. "Have you told Tucker yet?"

"No, I was going to call him later. I don't think it will matter to him where I live."

"You're wrong about that."

"Oh, and why is that, Mr. Sherlock Holmes?"

"You aren't his sister, but I could tell he has strong feelings for you."

Chapter Thirteen

"Do you have plans for tonight?" Caralyn asked.

"I was going to relax and watch a movie. Why?"

"I want to see you. I'll come to your place, and we can order a pizza."

"Okay, but I might not be very good company. I'm tired and my back is sore from a fall the other day at practice."

"I could give you a back rub if it would help," she offered.

"I'll see. What time are you coming?"

She checked the clock in her kitchen. "Would six be okay. I need to pay my bills and start a load of laundry."

"Six is fine. Should I order the usual and have it delivered?" He opened a drawer and pulled out the menu.

"Surprise me," she said. "But no anchovies, please. I'll see you later."

"Okay, a chicken pineapple pizza with extra anchovies and eggplant." he teased.

"I will bring my own dinner if that's how you are going to be."

"See you when you get here," he said with a chuckle.

"Dinner's here," Tucker said.

Caralyn jumped up from the couch and followed him into the kitchen. "Smells good. What did you order?"

"Pepperoni with veggies. Onions, mushrooms, green peppers and both green and black olives. You can pick off the green ones if you want."

"Why? I like them better." She opened a second smaller box. "Good. You ordered breadsticks, too."

"With garlic. You may want to brush your teeth after we eat," he said while getting plates from the cabinet.

"What do you have to drink?" She opened the fridge and looked. "I see a Coke. Do you mind if I drink it?"

"Go ahead. I'm sticking to water and energy drinks."

"Don't those taste like crap?" she asked opening the can.

"They aren't supposed to taste good. They're supposed to replenish electrolytes."

"Can we sit on the couch to eat? I want to watch a movie or something." She didn't wait for an answer. She plopped down on the couch Indian-style and took a bite of the garlic bread. "Do you have any new movies?"

"There are two new ones from Netflix. I was going to watch them tomorrow, but we can watch one tonight."

"Can't we watch both?" she asked taking a bite of pizza. "This is good. It's the sauce that sets their pizza apart."

"Franco claims it's the secret ingredients."

"What secret ingredients?" she asked looking at the movies. "This one first." She handed it to Tucker.

"If I told you it wouldn't be a secret, you goof."

She stuck out her tongue. "Can we watch both movies?"

"No, because you will fall asleep, and I'll have to carry you to bed."

She grinned.

"The guest bed."

"I promise not to fall asleep."

"I've heard that before." He started the DVD.

"Do you want the last slice?" she asked. "I'm full. Eat the last one, so I can put the box in the trash.

"I'll take it."

She cleaned up and sat beside him on the couch. "I need to tell you something, Tuck."

"What?" he asked as the credits played.

"I'm moving back home at the end of the month."

"Why?" he asked with a mouthful of pizza. "I thought you were looking for a job in the city."

"I was, but nothing came up. I want to move into Grandma's house..."

"It's your house now, Cara. Yours and Beth's."

"I liked living in the city, but I need to go back. Stockton Woods is my real home."

103

He stared at her.

"Yeah, I used to say I couldn't wait to leave, but now I realize how much I love living there."

"Did you tell Mom and Dad? What about your new friend? What was his name?"

"Te'von, and yes I told everyone. Te'von wants to live in New York City, so I broke off our relationship."

"Really?"

She smacked his arm. "It wasn't that kind of relationship." We were just friends."

"I bet he didn't know that."

"I've known him over a year, and we were always friends. We thought there might be something worth exploring, but it fizzled out."

"Is that what young ladies call it now? It used to be called hooking up or..."

"Hush, dork breath. I have never called it hooking up. That must be a guy thing."

"Let me know if you need help with your move."

She turned to face him. "So, you don't care if I move away, huh?"

"It's your life, Cara. You are supposedly an adult now. You can make those decisions on your own."

Midway through the second movie, Tucker noticed she was sound asleep. Rather than wake her up and send her home alone, he carried her to the spare bedroom and set her on the bed.

"You can get undressed if you wake up," he said as he moved her hair away from her face.

She woke up an hour later, saw the lights were still on in the living room, used the bathroom and headed back to the couch.

He saw her coming and said, "I thought you were out for the night."

"I woke up to pee. Do you want me to stay or go home?" She sat at the end of the couch and put her feet in his lap.

He massaged a foot out of habit. "It's up to you. I don't mind if you stay. It's pretty late for you to go home alone."

"I'll crash here if you don't mind. I still have toiletries in the guest bathroom, right?"

"I haven't thrown anything out. You have a change of clothes in the dresser from our days at MCU."

"Can I borrow a t-shirt to sleep in? It's either that or my underwear."

"Do you know where I keep them?" he asked without taking his eyes off the TV.

"I'll find one."

She borrowed a Bulls t-shirt and rejoined him on the couch.

He glanced at her legs.

"It's long enough for a minidress," she said.

"You better not wear it in public."

"Yes, *Daddy*," she teased.

"The movers are coming in the morning," Caralyn told her mother over the phone.

"Did Tucker help you pack?" Mom asked.

"A little. I could stay till the end of the month, but I want to get home before Halloween. It can be a little crazy here then."

"Davey volunteered to help the movers if you need him."

"I'll take him up on that," she replied.

"Have you heard anything from Derren lately?" Mom asked.

"Not in a while. Why? Have you heard anything? The last I knew, she was refusing to go to a counselor. Grandma will be upset if they get a divorce."

"We don't have to tell her," Mom said.

"I'm not going to lie to her if she asks about him. How is Melissa doing?"

"Okay, as far as I know. She is starting to show a little."

"Already? Maybe she's carrying twins."

Chapter Fourteen

"No! I'm not going to spend the whole weekend with your family," Natalie shouted.

"Why not? We were with your mother last weekend." Derren stood in the doorway of their bedroom with a hand on his hip. "We even went to Birmingham to visit your father in August. Why can't we visit my family? We don't even have to spend the night."

"If you want to go, fine. Go ahead. I have too much to do to spend the weekend visiting people."

"You use that lame excuse every week. I don't know what you have to do that is so important. Why can't it be done during the week in the evenings?"

"Because I am too tired and stressed. I need to unwind in the evenings."

Derren sighed and walked away. "I'm going to see my parents, and if they ask where you are, I'm not going to cover for you. I will tell them you aren't interested in seeing them."

"I don't care."

Derren gathered his coat, keys and wallet and left the house.

"Hello, is anyone home?" Derren walked into his parents' house. He set his keys on the red countertop, hung his coat on a hook by the back door and peeked into the living room. "There you are."

"Sorry, Derren. I didn't hear you."

"It's okay, Dad. Don't get up. Where's Mom?"

"She ran into town for groceries." He got up from his favorite chair anyway. "Did you come alone? Were we expecting you?"

"Yeah, Natalie was busy. She said to say hi. I didn't tell Mom we were coming. It was a spur of the moment decision."

Dad looked at his oldest son. "It's all right. Anything new happening at school?"

Derren sat on one of the chairs by the picture window, glanced outside for a moment before answering, "Not really. Our football team is undefeated. We might have a chance to go deep into the playoffs this year. We have a really good quarterback and a couple other decent players."

"That's good."

"Have you seen Davey this week? How is Melissa doing?"

"He and Melissa stopped by Wednesday night. She's doing all right. She complained about morning sickness. I remember when your mother was expecting you boys. She would get violently sick for about a week, but then it would be all over."

Dad talked about when Derren and Davey were young for a few minutes.

"Derren, are you here?" Mom asked as she walked in the back door. "Did Natalie come with you? I can make dinner."

"It's just me, Mom. Are there more groceries in the car?"

"A few bags."

"I'll get them for you. Dad fell asleep."

"He does that a lot more often now. There is ice cream in one of the bags. Would you put it in the freezer for me, please?"

Derren brought in the remaining bags and helped his mother put the groceries away.

"Have you brought up the subject of counseling to Natalie anymore?" Mom asked.

"I did, but she refuses to consider it." He smiled because she purchased two cans of Spam. "Does Dad still like this?"

"He likes it, but it causes heartburn. I'm not sure if it's the Spam or the fried onions. Sometimes I grind it up and make ham salad for sandwiches out of it."

"I don't suppose it's any worse for him than fried bologna."

"I haven't made that in years. When you and Davey were kids, I made it because it was cheap."

"Dad was telling me the tractor broke down again. Is he going to fix it? It might not be worth it."

"He talked about selling it if he can get it running. He told Garrett Reid he would let him farm the front forty acres next year."

107

"That's a good idea. Dad can work part-time at the Post Office. He likes it, and it's not as hard on him."

"He's like Grandpa Stanfield. He always has to be fixing something or going to auctions and estate sales."

Derren walked into the side room off the dining area. "He should read more books. He must have a couple thousand." He picked up an old hardcover from the desk. "Where did he find this?"

"An estate auction in Butler. Is it worth anything?"

Derren inspected the book. "It's an old western by James Will. If it was a first edition, it would be worth beaucoup bucks. This is a third printing. It's not worth more than a couple dollars."

"Your father likes old westerns. He gets that from your grandfather."

After supper Derren helped his mother with the dishes.

"Your aunt Sarah told me Caralyn is moving home this month. She mentioned something about Caralyn working on a novel."

"I'm not sure if I'm surprised or not. She finished grad school and was looking for a job."

"Sarah said Caralyn was upset because Tucker moved to a different apartment building."

Derren grunted. "I didn't know he moved. I've been pretty bad about keeping in touch."

"Is it because you don't want them to know about your issues with Natalie?" Mom washed the last plate and set in in the counter.

"They know we're struggling."

"Since your father is watching TV, let's sit in the kitchen and talk," Mom suggested.

They sat and listened to Carlton laughing at the antics of the Marx Brothers.

"He loves those old movies," Derren said.

"Be honest with me, son. Did you ever think Natalie would be so controlling?"

Derren sighed and stared at the ceiling for a moment. "I knew her mother was like that, and I could see it in Natalie to a degree, but nothing like now. When we were in college, she always wanted me to visit her. She resisted coming up to MCU. I put it down to her not wanting to be around the guys."

"Didn't she get along with Tucker and Caralyn?"

He flipped a hand back and forth. "Most of the time, but she had her own friends. Even in high school Natalie and Caralyn weren't real close. Please don't ever tell her, but Natalie thought Caralyn was immature and spoiled by the McKays and Grandpa and Grandma."

"She was spoiled by the Stanfields and my parents, too."

"Natalie was jealous of Cara, too. Her mother told her about the trust fund and that bothered Natalie."

"Didn't she realize Cara lost her parents in that accident?"

"She knew it, but she was still envious. She's always pushed me to look for a better job."

"I thought you like your job."

"I do, and the school district is above average, but she wants me to look into other professions to make more money."

"I never realized she was so materialistic," Mom said.

They chuckled as Derren's father slapped his knee and howled at a scene he had watched a dozen times or more.

Chapter Fifteen

"Could you put the couch against that wall, please?" Caralyn asked the movers.

"Where does this end table go?" Davey asked.

"In my bedroom," she answered.

Caralyn watched as all her worldly possessions came off the truck and were moved into the house where she had lived as a child with Grandma Florence Jackson.

Mom McKay was busy in the kitchen, but walked into the living room holding a ten inch frying pan.

"Do you really need three frying pans this size. This one was already here, but the other two came from Chicago."

"I tried to sell everything I could if I already had one here. No one wanted that one."

"Does it have any sentimental value?" Mom asked.

Caralyn shrugged and answered, "It's just an old pan. We can donate it to Goodwill or something." She watched as the movers brought in two recliners and told the guys where to place them. She looked at Mom and said, "I hope everything fits. I sold or got rid of stuff I knew I wouldn't need. My apartment was bigger than the house."

"Some things can go in the garage."

Caralyn nodded. "I am so glad we built a new one. The old garage wasn't worth fixing up, but I have a lot of memories about it."

"You and Tucker would use it as your fort when you were kids."

Caralyn laughed and added, "I loved the gravel floor. I thought all garages were like that. The new one is so nice. I could add a furnace and live in it."

"You might miss having running water," Davey said. "This box is labeled den. Which room is the den?"

"Oh, it can go in the back bedroom. I'm going to use it as a temporary office until I can figure out what to do. I would like to have a guest bedroom."

"Your grandfather did want to expand the house."

"Really?" Caralyn asked.

"He talked about it with Douglas and Jim before he died." Mom pointed out the window. "There's plenty of room between our houses. He talked about adding a new bathroom and two bedrooms."

"How would you get to the addition?" Davey asked. He set the box on the floor. "I don't want to hold it until you build the addition."

"You're a goof, Davey," Caralyn said with a laugh. "That's a good question."

"The plan was to put a doorway right there." Mom pointed to the corner of the living room. There's enough space in here. You could keep your furniture in this area and this part could be like a hallway without walls. An open space, I mean."

"Am I too late to help with the movers?" Dad McKay asked as he entered the kitchen.

"We are in here, Jim."

He walked into the living room.

"You aren't supposed to help," Caralyn said. "I'm paying these big strong men for that."

"Do you mean I get paid for working my butt off?" Davey asked grinning.

Caralyn poked his side. "Not you. I meant the other men. You're family and my absolute favorite cousin. You have to help me."

"Flattery will not work on me, Cara. Cold cash will though."

"Caralyn needs more space, and I was telling her about the addition Glen was thinking about before he... you know," Mom said.

"That's right, Cara. I haven't thought about that in years, but he actually had a set of plans. He knew how to do that kind of stuff. He was planning to build the addition with help from me, Douglas and your uncles. After he passed away, the plans were forgotten and never mentioned."

"Was this after the accident?" Caralyn asked without thinking.

"No, Cara, your grandfather died shortly after Beth was born," Mom reminded her.

Caralyn slapped her thigh. "I knew that. What was I thinking?" She looked out the window. "I never thought about adding on to the house, but it would make sense. Would it cost a lot?"

Dad rubbed his jaw. "We could save money if..."

"No! If it happens, I could use some of the trust money. It's not that I doubt the family's ability or skill, but everyone is older now and the cousins have lives of their own. If it happens, I want to hire people."

"It would be a chance to update the whole house. You could live with us while your house is remodeled," Mom said.

"Let me think about it," Caralyn said. "I still want this to be the house I grew up in, but it would be nice if it was bigger. I might want to get married and start a family someday."

"How was your week, Daddy?" Caralyn asked as she made soup for lunch a week after moving into her house.

"Students are getting younger every year," he replied. "How was your week? Did you do any work on your book?"

"I wrote three more chapters and revised a couple others."

"Have you unpacked everything?" Mom asked.

"Not even close," Caralyn said. "I still have boxes in my closet that I haven't touched."

"Have you thought about the addition?"

Caralyn turned from the stove still holding a spoon. "Yes! I talked to Mr. Dunlap at the lumber yard. I showed him Grandpa's plans and he came up with an estimate for the material and labor. It's expensive, but I think it would be worth it."

"Have you made a decision? Have you talked to Beth about it?" Dad asked.

"I called her Thursday and told her everything. She told me to go ahead if I want, so I want to do it."

112

"You will need to get a move on if you want to get the foundation work done before winter. Once that's done the framing and other work can be completed no matter the weather."

"Do you have time to talk to Mr. Dunlap with me this afternoon?" Caralyn asked.

"I will make time."

"Thank you, Daddy. I will learn how to build an addition."

Contracts were signed and the work on the addition began the following week. Caralyn and Mom watched as the excavating began.

"There will be less yard to mow," Mom said.

"I didn't think about that," Caralyn said as she took photographs. "I want to have photos of the work as it progresses. I am going to replace the roof since the guys will be doing the addition."

"Jim said it was close to time to replace it. It makes sense not to do it in sections."

"I might consider vinyl siding later, but for now I want to paint it like the rest of the house. A white house with gray trim and shutters looks good to me."

"Tucker, are you mad because I won't be at the game tonight?" Caralyn asked. "I would have come up, but I need to be here in case the guys have any questions about the addition."

"It's okay, Cara. I didn't expect you to drive up here for one game. We leave tomorrow for the coast and will be gone for a week."

"I hope you guys have a good year. If you make the playoffs, I will go to every game. That's a promise."

"I'll hold you to it. How's the work going? I saw the photos," he said while stuffing his duffel bag with essentials for his road trip.

"So far there haven't been any issues. Did I tell you I'm going to update the plumbing and electrical throughout the whole house?"

"Dad mentioned it. It shouldn't be too difficult because you have the basement. In the old part at least. Mom and Dad's house is on a crawlspace. There's not as much room to work."

"The addition is on a crawlspace, but I don't need more basement. The furnace and water heater and stuff are going to be changed. Replaced. They still work, but I want new ones."

"That's a good idea since you're doing it, you might as well go all the way."

"You know how the washer and dryer were in the basement, right?"

"I remember. Are you moving them?"

"I might keep the old ones down there, but I'm putting smaller units in the new bathroom. I thought about making the new bathroom part of the master bedroom, but that would mean revising the plans."

"What did you decide?"

"The door will be in the hallway."

"That will work."

"Oh, the guys are opening up the wall between the kitchen and dining room. It will make everything feel more spacious, but I don't know what to use the dining room for. It's a waste to put a table and buffet in there because it never gets used."

"I'm sure you will think of something, Cara. You're the creative one in the family."

"I better go. I hope you guys win and you stay safe. Don't get hurt."

He chuckled and said, "I'll try not to get in anyone's way."

Chapter Sixteen

"What did you do?" Caralyn asked. "I was watching the game, and you fell to the floor. Did you sprain an ankle, or did it break. It looked like you were in a lot of pain."

Tucker answered, "It's a high ankle sprain."

"Did they take x-rays?"

"Yes. Nothing broken, but the doctor said I would be out for two weeks. I've had sprains before, but this was worse. Before I would keep playing, but I can't do that at this level. I'm not as big or as strong as most of the guys in the league. If I can't rely on my quickness and mobility, I'm done."

"Then take the time to let it heal. That's an order, Tucker McKay."

He laughed and asked, "How's the work going? You didn't send any photos this week."

"Sorry. I will email them later."

"Are you staying in your house, or with Mom and Dad?"

"For now I'm staying in my house during the day to work, but sleeping in your old room. Do you mind?"

"It's been your room as much as mine over the years. I'm surprised Dad didn't build an addition, or move to a larger house long ago."

"I asked him, and he said there wasn't enough space on the side between houses, and the driveway was on the other side. The only way to add more room would have been to add a second story."

"Yeah, I suppose so, but they could have moved."

"I guess they never thought they would have a large family like most people in town."

"And it's a perfect location."

Caralyn laughed. "One of these days some developer will buy the land south of us and put in a neighborhood."

"Too bad it's not woods like at Uncle Carlton's place. It would be like living in the country."

"What do you mean you sprained the other ankle?" Caralyn asked. "You just got back after two weeks and now you..." She sighed and added, "This year isn't starting too well for you, or the team. Alphonse is the only guy who's playing well."

"I'm not the only guy who's hurt. We've had more nagging injuries this season than all of last year and it's still November."

"Speaking of November, are you coming to my surprise birthday party?"

"What surprise party? How can it be a surprise if you know about it?" he asked.

"It's a surprise because I'm throwing the party and not telling anyone until the morning," she answered.

Tucker laughed. "You are too funny, Cara. When is this party?"

"Have you forgotten when my birthday is? I still remember yours."

"Don't sound so disappointed. I know your birthday's November 30th. I just don't know day of the week it is."

"It's next Wednesday."

He checked his calendar. "Unless I can convince the Jazz to move the game to Illinois, I will be on a road trip. Sorry."

"You planned it so you would be gone, didn't you?" she asked sounding like a little girl.

"You got me there. I bribed whoever does the schedule to make sure the Bulls were nowhere near Chicago on that day."

"Okay, but you better call me and I'm not really having a party. Mom and Dad are busy, and it's the middle of the week. Everyone has to work."

"Speaking of work, are you still looking for employment?"

"I am self-employed."

"How?"

"I am an author and I do side jobs for people. Editing stuff. I even translated an article for one of my old professors."

"Old professor?"

"Ex-professor. He's in his forties."

Tucker asked, "Is he married?"

116

"Yes, and he has a mistress, too."

"Really?"

Caralyn laughed then shrugged. "I don't know. I said it to get a response. You better call me on my birthday, or else I won't let you see my new house."

"I will do my best to remember to call."

"Do you have to travel since you're injured?"

"Maybe not, but I have to go to therapy every day."

"Yeah, any excuse to stay away from me, huh?"

"Whatever it takes," he teased.

"I hate you, Tucker James. You better call me. I have to run. I have to decide how much of the wall between the kitchen and dining room I want to keep."

"Is this Caralyn Ann Dawson?" a voice on the phone asked.

"It is, but I'm not sure I recognize this voice. It kinda sounds familiar, but I can't put a face to it, since I haven't seen you in ages, Derren Stanfield. You are so mean to me."

"Sorry about that. Anyway, I have this day circled on my calendar for some reason. Do you have any idea why this day is special?"

"It's like the most important day of the year, Derry."

"I thought Christmas was next month."

She moved to the couch and put her feet on the coffee table. "Tell me how you and Natalie are doing? I won't take no for an answer. Tucker and I are concerned about it, and it's not because I'm nosy."

He chuckled and answered, "I know. I wish I could tell you more, but I don't know what to do. She refuses to see a counselor. She has threatened to file for a divorce, but hasn't yet. Not to my knowledge anyway."

"I can't understand why she changed so much. You guys were together all through high school and college. It's not like you rushed into marriage."

"I don't understand it either, but her mother doesn't make matters easier..."

117

"What did the old... What did she do now?"

"She got after Natalie for being indecisive about her future. It's like she's pushing for a divorce."

Caralyn sighed and got to her feet. "It's too bad you and Natalie can't divorce her mother."

"We could move to Idaho or somewhere she couldn't find us," Derren said with a laugh.

"That's a good idea. You could live on top of a mountain in a log cabin and grow a long beard and... whatever."

"I hope it doesn't come to that. I should let you go. Say hi to the McKays for me."

"I will, and we are praying for you and Natalie."

He raised his eyebrows, but said, "Thanks. I appreciate it."

"I just got home. Is it too late to meet you for dinner?" Richard asked.

"No, but where are you?" she asked with a grin.

"In my apartment. Aren't you in the city?"

"No! Why would I be there?"

"I thought you were going to celebrate your birthday with me. I was going to take you out for an expensive dinner... on the company of course. Then we would see a Broadway show. Go dancing afterward. Then I would bring you home and make love to you until the sun comes up and I have to head back to the office for another sixteen hour day."

"Could we skip the Broadway show and go straight to the lovemaking? I'd rather spend my birthday ravaging each other."

"If you insist, but I spent a fortune on tickets."

"It's only money. Wouldn't you rather spend the time with me?"

"Wait! Is this Debbie Delight?"

"Who's that?"

He shrugged and replied, "Just a name I thought of. Did you think she was a hooker?"

"With a name like that, she should be," Caralyn said then giggled. "Are you trying to tell me your sex life is suffering?"

"I might as well join a monastery and become a monk."

She put a finger to her mouth, moved to her bedroom and lay on the bed on her back. "That's a good idea, but I can't see you in one of those brown robes with a funny haircut like they have. But I guess it would be better than suffering the way you are."

"I met a lady at the office, and we talked, but neither one of us has time to go out for dinner or anything."

"Aw! You're leading the perfect life. You're working for a prestigious firm, in the most fascinating city in the states and meeting hundreds of beautiful women."

"Knock it off. If I wasn't a member of the New York bar, I would move to Stockton Woods and pursue a life of misery with you."

"We would make each other miserable because you would know how close I was, but still so far away from your bed."

"You have such a way with words. Have you ever considered becoming an author?" he teased.

"What? Give up my career as a... what do you call the ladies who have phone sex for money?"

"I don't know because I've never used that service."

"Just checking if you've stooped that low."

"Since you have such a unique way with words, how much would you charge for phone sex?"

She giggled. "Trust me. You couldn't afford it."

"Do you have like a sample session?"

"No, and have you talked to Derren lately?"

"I called him once this month, but he couldn't talk long. Natalie found out who was on the phone and demanded he help clean the kitchen. I feel bad, but he has to do something."

"He won't. He will suffer in silence for eternity before he admits it was a mistake."

"None of us saw this coming. I didn't. Did you?"

"No. No one did. I talked to him earlier today. He sounded so sad. I wish we could have the old Derren back."

"Have you talked to Tucker today?"

"He's going to call me around ten."

"I should let you go unless you want to talk dirty."

"Tell me your credit card number? I can run it to the limit."

"Are you that good?"

"Number first. Then you'll find out," she teased. "Try to take a couple hours off this month. You can't spend your whole life in the office."

"I'm sorry, Cara. I got busy and lost track of time. How has your day been?"

"Just like any other day except I talked to Richard and Derren." She told him about those calls.

"He's always going to flirt with you, huh?"

"I would worry if he didn't. I am concerned about Derren."

"We all are, but there's a section in Matthew 6 that addresses worry." He read it to her.

"I suppose. But as humans we tend to worry."

"You have to remember God is in control. We can rely on Him to provide our needs and care for us."

She stared at the phone as Tucker continued. *I don't think this religion thing is a fad with you. You've been changed, and I need to pursue the kind of relationship you have with Jesus.*

"All we can do is pray, Cara. God will do the work," he said then paused.

"I promise to pray more for them. I will."

"It's good to hear your voice, Carrie. I miss you."

"I miss you, too, Bubby," she said with her voice choking. After a moment she asked, "Have you met any charming ladies?"

"What?"

"It's been five months."

"No!"

"Too soon, huh?"

"Yes, it's too soon. How could you even think I would be ready to start dating? That's out of line, Caralyn." he ended the call.

"Crap! I really blew it," she muttered.

120

Chapter Seventeen

"Tucker said to tell you hi," Mom said. She looked at Caralyn who was working on her laptop in the living room. "Did you have an argument or something. I offered to let him talk to you, but he said he needed to run. What's going on?" She sat next to Caralyn. "You can tell me anything."

Caralyn closed her laptop, sighed and said, "He called on my birthday and everything was fine. We talked about stuff and said we missed each other. Then I screwed up royally."

"How?"

"I asked him if he's met anyone." Caralyn looked at Mom and chewed her lip. "He got mad and I haven't talked to him since. I left a message telling him I was sorry, and he replied that he was sorry for hanging up, but we haven't talked, texted or anything since then. I was insensitive and should have known it's too soon for him to think about someone else."

"You're right about that," Mom said. "But you can't stop talking to each other like the time you were in France."

"I know, but he doesn't want to hear from me yet."

"Are you sure?"

"Pretty sure."

Mom stood up. "He's playing tonight. I heard it on the Butler radio station. You might want to watch the game."

"I will."

"He apologized because the team will be on the road through Christmas. It's the first time he won't be home for the holidays."

"Is he staying away because of me? They can't have a game every night."

"He won't admit it, but it could be part of the reason."

"We could drive to the city and surprise him," Caralyn suggested.

"I don't think he's ready for a surprise, but we could ask if he'd like some company."

"Hi, Davey. What brings you to town?" Caralyn asked while cleaning up the kitchen after dinner.

"I wanted to see how the house is progressing." He looked out the window and pointed to the addition. "It looks weather tight. The windows are in, and the roof looks good."

"They did the whole roof. The guys left already. Would you like a tour, or do you need to get home?"

"Melissa's at her parents. I want a full tour."

"Let me finish this. Talk to your uncle about school while I finish. He is being a curmudgeon about something the college administration did, but won't tell us."

Davey tilted his head. "I thought a curmudgeon was a fish."

"Go! Talk to him before I smack you."

"Did you decide to go ahead with the vinyl siding on the whole house?" Davey asked. "You can't paint in winter."

"Mr. Dunlap convinced me to do it. The trim and shutters will still be wood, but they get finished in the factory or wherever. I was going to do it eventually, so I decided to do it now instead of paying for painters now and... you know what I mean." She nudged his hip with hers because he was laughing at her. "Hey! I'm a girl. I didn't know anything about building a house before this."

"I give you credit for taking on the responsibility. You know what you want and are making sure you get it."

"Thanks. Can we go inside before I freeze to death?"

"There's this thing called a coat," he teased as he followed her up the porch steps and into the kitchen.

"Shut up, creepo."

"What are you doing to the kitchen?"

"Tearing out that wall. Most of it anyway. It's not a supporting wall, and it will open everything up."

"Are you going to actually use the dining room as a dining room. You have a table in the kitchen."

"Not all the time but occasionally."

He checked the partially demoed wall. "Why are you leaving a partial wall?"

"It will be a place to hang decorations, and I'm not sure about the dining room. I wish it was like Mom and Dad's house where the living room and dining room are essentially one big open room. Here they are at an angle, and I can't change that without doing a lot more than I want to. Money wise, I mean."

"Yeah, I see what you mean. Too bad the porch and living room weren't switched."

"I might see if that wall can be removed." She touched the wall that separated the dining room from the hallway. "It would really open things up if it can go away. I would need to have the hardwood floor refinished."

"That's not that difficult. I could handle it."

"I haven't decided. Mr. Dunlap said the front door could be moved to here. I could close off the living room with French doors and use it as a family room..."

"For yourself?"

She smacked his arm. "I might have a family someday."

"I'm teasing. Continue the tour, please."

"I feel so confused because of the dining room. Anyway, the two old bedrooms are staying as is. I want to update the old bathroom at some point. Not yet though."

"Will there be a door separating the old house from the addition?"

She shook her head. "I want it to be open. Follow me, sir." She took his hand and pulled him along. "The walls are studded, but the drywall can't go up until the electric and stuff... you know what has to happen. Don't make fun of me."

"What is this room going to be?"

She grinned and said, "For now it will be my office. This is where I will write my novels and when I get old, I will sit in a rocker and knit sweaters for all my grandkids."

"You're a goof, Cara."

"And you're a creepo."

He walked down the hall. "Bathroom?"

"Yes, and the master bedroom is there. There is going to be a walk-in closet. That's it. What do you think?"

"You're going to have a beautiful home, Carrie."

She grinned and hugged him. "Thank you, Davey."

"One question."

"What?"

"Is this a doorway? Isn't there one right there?"

"Yes, and the reason is if I ever have a baby, and that becomes the nursery, I don't want to have to walk all the way around to get into the room. Doesn't that makes sense?"

"I guess so."

She walked into her old bedroom. "With a door on this side, whoever is using this room is right across the hall from the bathroom."

"But your old bathroom is at the end of the other hallway. It's close enough."

"Don't give me a hard time, Davey. It's where one of the windows was. So it was easy to turn it into a door."

"What happened to the siding?" He pounded on the new drywall.

"It couldn't be salvaged. I lost the windows in the old bedrooms."

"You still have one in your grandmother's old room. It opens to the porch, right?"

"Yes, but there used to be windows on this side." She looked at him and saw him grin. "I should smack you."

"I guess you can't have a window in an interior room."

"It is strange to have a bedroom without a window, but it could be my office or a den."

"Whatever you decide to do, should be okay, Cara. Do you have an idea of when it will all be finished?"

She crossed her fingers. "Unless something happens, it should be completely finished by the end of February."

Chapter Eighteen

"The painters finished yesterday, and I've spent most of the day cleaning and arranging things," Caralyn told Mom McKay on the phone. She removed the red bandana from her forehead and shook her hair free. "If you give me thirty minutes to shower, I will give you a tour. I could even make dinner if you like."

"Your father requested homemade chicken noodle soup. I think he's coming down with a cold, and the soup is his medicine. We can share if you'd like."

"Thanks. I will. Give me some time and come on over. I am thrilled by how the house turned out."

Mom smiled and said, "I can hear it in your voice, Cara. We will be there soon."

Caralyn showered, got dressed and ran around the house making sure everything looked perfect. The doorbell rang, and she took one last look before opening the door.

"Welcome to my new home."

"Thank you for inviting us." Mom held a pot of homemade chicken noodle soup.

"Let me take that." Caralyn took the pot.

"It's hot."

"I will be careful. Give me a sec and I'll give you the tour." She moved through the dining room, saw one of the pictures on the wall was crooked and set the soup on the stove.

Dad McKay peeked into the new addition. "It's almost hard to tell the difference between the old floor and the new one. Whoever refinished the hardwood did a good job."

"I love the paint color. Using the same color in the living room, dining room and hallway was a good choice," Mom said.

Caralyn adjusted the picture and rejoined her parents. "What do you think so far. I know you've seen it as the guys were working, but it's all finished now."

"Show us the new part first," Mom said.

Caralyn curtsied and said, "Right this way, please."

They followed Caralyn into her office.

"I like how you have your desk in front of the large window. You can see outside as you work." Mom smiled when she saw a photograph on the desk of the *family* together when Caralyn was thirteen. She did an about-face. "You have your work area and an area for conversation."

"Is this new furniture?" Dad asked as he sat in one of the large leather chairs. "Nice! It's a recliner."

"It's new to me," Caralyn answered. "I found it at that place in Butler. It's looks almost brand new, but I saved a bunch of money."

"I like the book shelves." Dad got up and looked at the books. "Did Davey build these for you?"

"He suggested the built-ins and did a great job building them. He made them look like they've been here for fifty years."

They left the office and moved down the hall.

"I like the fact I can close my office off from the rest of the house. It won't always be as clean and organized."

"Your bathroom looks bright and inviting." Mom picked up the towel Caralyn had left on the floor and hung it up on the towel rack. "It was a great idea to put a washer and dryer in here."

"This one makes the other bathroom look disgusting. I will update it at some point."

"Wow! Your bedroom is bigger than ours." Dad stretched out his arms. "I'm jealous."

Caralyn opened the closet door. "You don't have one of these."

Mom walked into the closet. "Jim, you need to figure out a way to expand our house. I must have a walk-in closet."

"We could convert the second bedroom into a large closet."

"Dad, you can't do that. Tucker needs a place to stay when he's home."

"Couldn't he stay with you?" Dad asked. "You have extra bedrooms."

"He might not want to," Caralyn answered. "I want to show you the old part. The guys did a great job with the crown molding and updating the kitchen."

"Kitchens are expensive to remodel," Mom said. "I would like to do ours, but it's too small to bother with."

"The kitchen still looks like Grandma's in a way, but better."

"This is new." Dad opened a door and walked into what was Caralyn's old bedroom.

"The door is where one of the windows used to be. I wanted one here because the bathroom is across the hall."

"And your new bedroom is close," Mom added.

"I wondered where you put the TV." Dad leaned on the back of one of the old chairs and looked at the TV and audio gear.

"I didn't want it to be in the living room anymore. This room can be a third bedroom if I ever need one." She looked at Mom and chewed her lip for a split-second.

They walked through the TV room and across the hall into the dining room.

Dad slapped the wall. "Too bad this couldn't be removed. It would really open up the house."

"Mr. Dunlap said it's a support wall, but it could be removed if I put a steel beam there. It would have been a lot of work and costs quite a bit. I decided to leave it as is. I'm used to it and it gives me a place to put photos and the buffet."

"I should warm up the soup." Mom went into the kitchen and turned on the burner. She stirred the soup then turned around. "I see what you mean. I can still picture Florence's kitchen, but it looks new in a way. I like the light yellow color. She always said a yellow kitchen made her think of sunshine."

Dad opened the fridge. "Is this new? Didn't it used to be over there?"

"It's new and it used to be by the door. The guys built that bench and now I have a place for coats and boots and stuff right inside the door. Grandma used to get on me because I would come inside and track dirt and mud on her floor. Now there"s a place to remove your shoes and sit down to do it."

"I like it, Cara. You have plenty of room in here even with the table."

"Thanks, Mom. I thought about putting in an island and getting a smaller table, but decided it would change the feel of the room too much."

Dad checked the floor. "I like how the floor transitions from hardwood to the new tile in the kitchen. What are your plans for the dining room?"

Caralyn put her hands on her hips. "I don't know. It won't get used that often."

"It will be nice when the whole family is here. Cousins, aunts, uncles and grandparents, I mean." Mom turned off the soup. "We can eat whenever you're ready."

Dad ran a hand over the table. "I remember going to my grandparents house when I was a kid. They liked to do these big puzzles. They would set them on the dining room table and cover them with a pad of some sort if they needed to eat in there."

Caralyn grinned and asked, "Do you want to use it for puzzles? You can if you want."

"No, I was simply reminiscing. Let's eat. I need my cold medicine."

"Hey, Caralyn, I figured I better call you..."

"Did Melissa have the baby? Is she okay? How's the baby? I have to see her right away."

Davey laughed and said, "Yes to all your questions. Everyone is doing fine, and we named her Lyndsey June. Before you ask June is Melissa's grandmother's name."

"I still have a hard time believing you're going to be a father."

"Why? Do you still think of me as a kid you like?" he teased.

"I'm not a kid, you dork brain. I've finished college and own my own house. Half of it at least."

"Did you and Beth split the house in two. Do you own the new part and she owns the rest?"

"You're a real riot. Would it be all right if I come up to the hospital in the morning?"

"Sure. She's in room 410. Mom and Dad got here a few minutes ago."

"Is Uncle Carlton happy to be a grandfather?" Caralyn asked.

Davey laughed. "You should see him. He's holding her and talking like she can understand him. He claims she can already recognize him and that she smiles at his lame jokes."

"Mom told me he was like that when I was a baby. He would stop by the house after he finished his bus route and play with me."

"Yeah. Dad's always liked you for some reason. He's kinda strange that way."

"Shut up before I tell your parents about the naughty things you used to do to me."

"Like I was the one who did all that stuff."

"I'll see you in the morning. Have you called Mom?"

"Not yet."

"Don't bother. I'll tell her. She just got home from school. See ya."

Caralyn raced out the door, across the yard and bounded onto the porch and walked in. "Melissa had the baby this afternoon. I'm going to see her in the morning."

"Are they doing all right?" Mom set her book bag on the table and quickly sorted the mail.

"They're okay. Her name is Lyndsey June."

"That's a nice name. Her grandmother was named June."

Caralyn followed her mother into the kitchen and sat at the table. "Can I tell you something important without you getting all judgmental?"

"Of course, sweetie. Would you like some tea? I'm going to make myself a cup."

Caralyn waved. "I'm good."

"What do you need to tell me?" Mom chose a tea and added water to the coffee maker.

"I want to start a family."

"You do, huh?"

129

"I don't mean like today, but I don't want to wait too long."

Mom leaned against the counter and stared at Caralyn. "You're serious."

Caralyn nodded. "I know I'm putting the cart before the horse since I don't even have a boyfriend."

"I was wondering if you had a father picked out, and does he know about your plans?"

"That's just it. There isn't anyone, and there aren't too many choices in Stockton Woods."

"There aren't too many eligible men worth consideration in the entire county," Mom said with a laugh.

"I might have to search the entire southern part of the state." Caralyn put a hand to her face. "I better start a search on the computer."

"I've heard some people even get married before they start a family," Mom teased.

"Would it bring shame to the family if I had a baby before I got married?"

Mom sat next to Caralyn and took her hand. "I would never be ashamed of you, but it might take your father a while to get used to the idea."

Caralyn's shoulders slumped and she put her elbows on the table and her chin in her hands. "He would definitely freak."

"You aren't..."

"No way. It's been... you know... a long time."

Chapter Nineteen

"Knock! Knock! Is anyone home?" Caralyn peeked around the partially open door.

Suddenly, Davey opened the door.

Caralyn jumped. "You scared me, creepo." She smacked his arm. "Can I come in?"

"I suppose since you're already here." He stepped out of the way and opened the door wider. "Lyndsey just finished eating and Melissa is in the bathroom."

Caralyn wrinkled her nose. "TMI, Davey." She peered into the bassinet at Lyndsey. "She's sleeping."

"Yep! That's what she does. She sleeps, eats and poops. Then she wakes up and repeats everything."

"She's a baby. What did you expect her to do?"

"She likes it when I hold her."

Caralyn snorted. "How do you know? Did she smile and make goo goo noises?"

"I'm her father. I can tell those things."

"You're a doofus."

They turned when they heard the toilet flush and a moment later Melissa walked out of the bathroom.

"She looks beautiful. Can I hold her if she wakes up before I leave?" Caralyn asked.

"Sure. She might sleep for an hour though," Melissa replied.

"Cara, have you had lunch? I haven't eaten since dinner and I'm starving. Care to grab a bite? Lyndsey might be awake then."

"Are you buying, Davey?"

He shrugged. "I can't. I just had a baby and the bills are already pouring in. Did you know the hospital charges you by the second?"

"Get out!"

"True."

"I don't believe you, and I'll buy. Where should we go? Don't say the cafeteria because I'm not eating hospital food."

"You're buying, so you can choose, but I like..."

"If I have to buy, we're eating at the Dairy King. It's close and cheap."

"She's is such a sweetheart and so tiny. I'm afraid I will break her if I hold her too tight," Caralyn said.

"She won't break," Davey said with a laugh.

"Have you dropped her already?" Caralyn frowned at him. "You better be careful with her."

"I haven't dropped her, and I am very gentle when I hold her."

"I think she's hungry," Caralyn said a few minutes later when Lyndsey began to fuss. "You can have her back, and I should get going. Let me know if you need any help."

"I could use your help at the farm."

"Not a chance, Davey. That reminds me, I'm going to stop and see Grandma and Grandpa. She wants me to help clean the house." Caralyn grabbed her purse and coat.

Davey walked her to the door. "Tell them hi, and I'll bring everyone to see them soon."

Caralyn parked close to the corn crib and headed inside. As she opened the gate to the yard surrounding the house, she saw her grandparents outside. She ran to them, and Grandma looked up and smiled.

"Grandma, why are you working outside?"

"It's warm enough and I want to get my flowerbeds ready for spring."

Caralyn hugged them both. "Let me do that. You shouldn't be working so hard."

Grandpa Stanfield handed Caralyn the hoe, but then clutched his chest.

"Clyde, what is the matter?" Grandma asked. "You look pale."

"My chest hurts..."

Caralyn waited by the front gate after calling 9-1-1. She heard the ambulance before she could see it. She raced to the gate which opened to the farm yard and waved as the ambulance slowed down.

"He's over here!" she shouted as soon as it stopped.

Kevin Jonas jumped out, grabbed some gear and followed Caralyn.

"What were you doing, Mr. Stanfield?" Kevin asked as his brother Richard came running up with a gurney.

"We were working on the flowerbed," Anna Stanfield answered. "He was okay, and then he grabbed his chest and said it hurt."

After checking vitals and making sure Mr. Stanfield was stable enough to transport, the volunteer paramedics loaded him onto the gurney.

"Should we follow you?" Caralyn asked.

"Yes. We should be at the hospital in ten minutes. The ER will be ready for him."

"Caralyn, do you always drive this fast?" Grandma held onto the door handle with one hand and used the other to brace herself.

"No, but I want to get there as quickly as we can."

"Please, don't have an accident. I don't think they have another ambulance to send if we do."

"I won't. I'm a good driver, Grandma."

Caralyn parked in the newly paved lot close to the ER.

"Do you know where to go?" Grandma asked.

Caralyn took her hand. "We will find him."

She walked up to the receptionist. "We're looking for..."

"Mrs. Stanfield, I will take you to your husband."

"Thank you."

The receptionist walked out from behind her desk. "You must be Caralyn Dawson. I know your mother. I'm Pola Bailey. We used to live down the street from the Boyds until we moved to Butler."

"I kinda remember you."

Mrs. Bailey opened a door and led them to a waiting area. "I will have the doctor talk to you as soon as he can."

"Thank you, Mrs. Bailey," Caralyn said. She sat beside Grandma and rubbed her back as Grandma wrung a hanky in her hands. "I'm sure Grandpa will be okay. He was talking to you before the guys put him in the ambulance."

"His doctor told him to be careful, but he doesn't listen."

A few minutes later a tall young man in a white lab coat approached. "Mrs. Stanfield, I am Dr. Bausch, and I treated your husband today. He is doing much better now, but I would like to keep him here so our cardiologist can run some tests."

"Did he have a heart attack?" Caralyn asked. "I'm Caralyn Dawson. Their granddaughter."

"Yes, I recognize you. My son, David, played basketball for Butler."

"I remember him."

"Mr. Stanfield didn't have a heart attack, but his heart is out of rhythm." He smiled and added, "We fixed it and he's been asking for you."

"Can we see him?" Caralyn asked excitedly.

"Yes. I will have the nurse take you to him. He will be moved to a regular room as soon as possible."

Caralyn held Grandma's hand as the nurse took them to Grandpa.

"Clyde, you scared the life out of me."

Caralyn watched as her grandparents showed more emotion toward each other than she had ever witnessed. *I don't think I've ever seen Grandpa cry.* She sat and listened as they talked softly to each other.

"Caralyn called for an ambulance right away. She knew exactly what to do."

Grandpa waved at Caralyn, and she stood by the edge of the bed.

"I'm sorry if I scared you, sweetie. I didn't mean to," he whispered.

134

"It's okay. I'm glad you're going to be all right."

"I want to go home."

Caralyn shook her head. "You can't go home today. The doctors want to keep you here to do some tests, and you have to follow their orders. The nurses will take good care of you."

"There's someone who wants to see you," Davey said as he stood in the doorway of Grandpa's hospital room.

Caralyn jumped up and moved quickly to the door. "Are you allowed to be here? Where's Melissa?"

"I'm right here," she said moving next to Davey and Lyndsey.

"How did you know we were here?"

"Caralyn, everyone knows Grandpa is here."

"I did call Mom, but I forgot to let everyone else know."

"Can I see her?" Grandma asked.

"Would you like to hold her?" Davey asked.

Grandma nodded and smiled. Davey brought Lyndsey to where she was sitting.

"She's so tiny, but she has good color."

"Are you going home?" Caralyn asked Davey.

"We are already discharged, but thought we should take time to see Grandma and Grandpa."

After holding the baby for several minutes, Grandma stood up. "Do you want to hold your first great-grandchild?"

Grandpa sat up a little higher in bed and held out his arms. "It's been a long time since I held a baby." He looked at Caralyn. "You were probably the last one I held since you're the youngest."

Grandma carefully placed Lyndsey in his arms.

"She's waking up. She's smiling at me now."

"That's because she knows you will spoil her," Caralyn said. "That's what grandpas do."

"I'm going to take Grandma home now," Caralyn said shortly before eight. "She wanted to stay, but I told her she needs to get a good night's sleep. I will bring her back in the morning."

135

"I will be ready to come home when you get back. Tell everyone thank you for coming to see me. They didn't need to bother."

Grandma stood up, leaned over and kissed him.

"Grandpa, you can't come home until the doctor says you can. You can't be stubborn either. You need to let the nurses take care of you."

"They wait until I fall asleep then they come in and wake me up. How can I get any rest?"

"You will get used to it."

Caralyn and Grandma had been waiting for an hour when Grandpa was wheeled back into the room the next morning.

"Did you pass your test?" Caralyn asked. She put down her book and helped him adjust his pillows.

"The doctor will let me know later. I feel good enough to go home, but the nurse said I have to stay."

Dr. Hausman walked into the room an hour later with a laptop.

"Can I go home now, doctor?" Grandpa asked.

"Clyde, I know you want to go home, but I need to run another test later. I need to make sure your ticker isn't going to go goofy again. You wouldn't want that to happen, would you?" He winked at Caralyn. "His heart is back to normal, but I want to keep him and run the test again. If that test is okay, I might let him out of here tomorrow afternoon. With one condition."

"What is that?" Grandma asked.

"He has to stay inside and rest for a week. Then I want to see him in my office. You aren't getting any younger, Clyde, and I want to keep you around a while longer. You're the only person I can beat at checkers."

Grandpa laughed. "Albert, I let you win a game once in a while so you'll keep playing."

"I thought I was letting you win," Dr. Hausman replied.

When Grandpa's heart rhythm fluctuated in the morning, Dr. Hausman ordered him to stay another night. It was Tuesday afternoon before the doctor was satisfied Grandpa's heart was going to stay in rhythm.

"I had my nurse make an appointment for you. Until then you better follow orders." Dr. Hausman pointed a finger. "Got that?"

"I will make sure he follows your orders," Caralyn said.

"You need to keep an eye on your grandmother and don't let her do too much. She's not getting any younger either." He did an about-face when he heard a familiar voice enter the room.

"My taxi is waiting outside. I hear I have a passenger waiting to go home."

Caralyn rolled her eyes. "Uncle Carlton, you use the same joke all the time."

"Why change them if they still get a laugh?" Carlton walked up to her and put an arm around her shoulders. "I hear you've been staying all day and only going home for a few hours to sleep. Is that true, little lady?"

"I wanted to make sure he didn't try to escape."

"Dad, are you ready to go home and start plowing the back forty?" Carlton asked shaking hands with Dr. Hausman. "After that you can help me paint the barn."

Caralyn and Grandma looked at each other and shrugged.

Chapter Twenty

"I hope I didn't interrupt your work," Mom said. "When I got home there was a message on the phone from Tucker."

"I was taking a break. I've been translating a manuscript into French. How's he doing?" Caralyn asked.

"He has two days off and is coming home."

"Really? It's about time he came home to see you. How long is he staying? Did he say when he would arrive?"

Mom checked the clock in the dining room. "He should be home for dinner. Didn't he call you?"

"No. Why?"

"In the message he mentioned taking you to dinner."

"Really?"

"Cara, I think he's embarrassed about ignoring you the last few months. I think he wants to apologize."

"He should. He acted like a jerk."

"Are you going to be gracious, or will you gloat and make it difficult?"

"I won't act like a jerk even though he might deserve it.

"I can throw a meat loaf together for tomorrow night, and I could make cheesy potatoes. He loves them."

"Sounds yummy. Did he say where he wants to take me?"

Mom tried to remember. "He didn't say, but probably somewhere in Butler. That would be more appropriate than The Curve, or the new cafe next to the grocery store."

"I'll clean up and be ready whenever he gets here."

"Be nice to him."

Caralyn rolled her eyes. "I'll be nice, but he better not treat me like a baby."

She showered and was working in her office when she saw Tucker pull into the driveway. *About time you came home, buster.* She watched him go inside then went back to work.

Fifteen minutes later she heard a knock on the door. She giggled and opened it.

"Yes. May I help you with something?"

Tucker sighed and said, "You're not gonna make this easy, are you?"

"Nope."

"Can I come in, or do I have to grovel on the porch?"

She put a finger to her mouth. "I suppose you can grovel inside." She moved aside and let him in. "You look familiar, but I can't remember your name."

"Mom said you would play this for all you could."

"And why not? You haven't talked to me for months, Tucker McKay, and the last time I saw you, you treated me like a jerk."

He waited for more, but she only frowned at him.

"Is that it? Can I apologize now?"

"Yes. You may grovel."

"I'm sorry I treated you like a jerk, Caralyn. Will you accept my apology?"

She tried to keep a frown on her face, but couldn't. She wrapped her arms around his neck and hugged him.

"Does this mean you accept my apology?"

"Hush. Mom said you want to take me to dinner."

"Can we go to The Curve?"

"Not a chance, buster. There's a new place in Butler I hear has excellent steaks. You are going to pay righteous bucks tonight."

"I deserve it." He squeezed her close and could smell the strawberry scented shampoo in her hair. "I missed you, Carrie. I've been kinda miserable lately. I hate my new apartment, but I couldn't stay..."

"I know, and me moving home didn't help. I should have stayed until you were through grieving."

"Do I get a tour before we leave?"

"You are in the living room..."

She showed him the addition.

"I like the color you chose for your bedroom." He touched the wall and looked at the bed.

"I'm glad you approve." She sat on the edge of the bed.

"Would it make any difference if I didn't like this peach color?"

"No, but I'm happy you like it. Are you ready to go? I'm getting mighty hungry. I might eat two steaks."

"Yeah, that'll be the day when you can eat more than one small steak."

She poked his side. "Are you driving, or do I have to?"

"I'll drive. I talked to Grandma, and she said you drove like a maniac on the way to the hospital."

"I got us there in one piece."

"Get your coat and let's go."

The hostess giggled when she saw Tucker and seated them at a booth along the side of the restaurant.

"Let me know if I can be of service. I'm Paige and your waitress will be Bianca."

"Thank you, Paige." Tucker smiled

Paige backed away and bumped into the table behind her. She turned and raced back to her station.

"Did you always get that reaction from high school girls, Mr. McKay?"

"She's older than high school, and she's probably a basketball fan," Tucker answered while checking the menu.

"I know what I want."

"How can you decide so fast, Cara?"

"They have a six ounce filet mignon with shrimp. I want that and a baked potato loaded with everything and a house salad with thousand island."

"Anything else?"

"A Dr Pepper to drink."

"Should I order for you, or do you want..."

"You can order. Bianca won't even know I'm here," Caralyn teased.

"I knew you'd need a box." Tucker grinned at Caralyn. "You did finish your salad and dinner roll."

140

"Hush. I might need a snack later. How was your steak? Did you see the look on Bianca's face when you ordered. I think she thought it was all for you. She didn't know I was here."

"My steak was delicious. I guess I might have to eat the rest of yours later."

"Not a chance."

Tucker paid the check, left a tip and they headed out to his car.

"Where to now?"

"Where would you like to go, Cara?" He opened the car door for her.

"Wow! You are being the gentleman tonight."

"Mom told me I have to be nice." He closed her door and got in on the other side.

"Can we go to Uncle Alton's lake? I know it's too cold to swim, but I like sitting on the dock."

"Okay, but don't blame me if you freeze."

"Won't you hold me if I get too cold?" She said in her childlike voice.

"Maybe."

"I've watched some of your games." Caralyn put her feet over the edge of the dock but kept them out of the water. "Your ankle seems a whole lot better."

"I have to soak it after every game, but it's good enough to play." He put an arm around her waist. "I was worried they might trade me or cut me."

"They can't do that if you're hurt, can they?"

"They can do whatever they like, but at least my contract is guaranteed. I would get paid no matter what."

She shifted her position and sat facing Tucker. "I can go to the cemetery tomorrow if you want. I won't listen if you talk to her."

"Thanks, but I stopped before I came home." He gazed out at the water. "Do you ever think about... blueberry scented candles?"

141

"Tucker James! Are you asking about the night we had sex?"

"Geez, Carrie, you don't have to be so blunt."

"Why not. I don't regret it, and you shouldn't either."

He leaned back using his hands for support. "I don't regret it, but I feel guilty about it because it was a sin."

"We didn't think of it like that. We did it because we wanted to. Maybe I wanted it more, but you could have said no."

He pulled her close and looked into her eyes for a moment.

"Kiss me, Tuck," she whispered and pulled his face to hers.

He kissed her quickly, then kissed her again.

"That wasn't a kiss of regret. You wanted to kiss me."

"I wanted to see if it still felt as good as before."

"Did it?" she asked then giggled.

He stood up and pulled her to her feet. "I'm taking you home, Cara." He put his arms around her waist.

She grinned and backed up against him. "You can take me home. I have my own bedroom. I have candles and we can have privacy."

He released her and backed away.

She faced him and asked, "Did I assume too much?"

"I'm sorry, but we can't go back to the way it was."

"Don't you want to?"

"That's just it. I want to very much, but I can't. I can't cause you to do something God doesn't want us to do."

"You're serious about this, huh?"

"It's the most serious thing I've ever done, Cara."

She shivered and whispered, "You better take me home. I'm getting chilled."

"Thanks for breakfast, Mom."

"You are welcome, Tucker. Do you have plans?"

"Cara and I are going to see if we can help Grandma with anything. Grandpa is still not supposed to do anything strenuous, and she said he wants to work in the machine shop on some projects."

142

"Caralyn is the only one he will listen to. Tell her to make sure he follows the doctor's orders."

"Okay. I'm not sure when we'll be back. Grandma will make lunch for us, but I'll try to be home for dinner."

"What time do you have to leave in the morning? Will you have time for breakfast?"

"I need to leave by eight. It was good to come home."

"I'm ready to go," Caralyn walked in as Tucker was hugging his mother. "Do I get a hug, too?"

"Sure. Mom can hug you," he teased.

She stuck out her tongue at him. "See you later, Mom."

"You don't have to do anything," Grandma said. "We will manage somehow."

"Grandma, you need to let us help you. Grandpa, you are still recovering. Don't you dare disobey me." She pointed a finger at him then put her hands on her hips. "What did Dr. Hausman tell you to do?"

"Take it easy and obey you."

"That's right. Tucker and I know what needs to be done. You lay on the couch and watch your shows. There's probably a rerun of *Gunsmoke* on."

Grandma handed Tucker a list of chores and small projects. "You don't have to do them all. Davey can do some of them."

Caralyn shook her head. "He has to take care of Lyndsey. Tucker will finish these, and I will make sure he does them right."

They worked until Grandma hollered for them to come in for lunch. By three o'clock everything on the list had been crossed off.

"We're done, Grandma. It didn't take as long as I thought. Tucker can work pretty hard when I make him," Caralyn teased.

"I don't know what I'd do without you kids. Let me give you some money."

"Grandma! You aren't paying us," Caralyn insisted.

"But I would have to pay someone to do it. It might as well be you." Grandma tried to give them each twenty dollars.

"We won't take your money," Tucker said with a laugh. "She didn't do enough to earn it, and I don't need the money. I'm a professional athlete, remember?"

"Did you go to the cemetery?" Grandma asked. "I know you talk to Nancy."

"I did."

"Have you talked to Derren lately? I worry about him and Natalie."

"I talked to him briefly last week. He's doing okay."

Grandma shook her head. "Don't you lie to me, young man. I know better."

"He and Natalie have been struggling," Caralyn said. "But I'm sure they will work it out."

"I wish that were true," Grandma said with a sigh.

"How much do you know?" Tucker asked.

"Maybe more than you. He stopped by and talked to us. I know she moved to Indiana."

Tucker looked at Caralyn then back at Grandma. "Derren said she wants a divorce, and he won't contest it. I'm sorry."

"He told me. I told him he shouldn't feel bad because he did everything he could to make the marriage work. I've seen it before."

"What, Grandma?"

"Sometimes people change for no good reason, sweetie. We may not understand it, but sometimes it's better to end the marriage."

"Did you ever feel that way about Grandpa?" Caralyn asked.

"Never. We've been married for sixty-eight years."

"That's a long time." Caralyn looked up at Tucker and grabbed his hand. *If we got married this year, it would take us until 2079 to match their achievement.*

"We're going to head home, Grandpa." Tucker smiled at him. "You take it easy. If you need anything done, call Davey or Caralyn. She makes a good supervisor. She watches and tells people if they aren't doing things right."

"Thank you for helping." Grandpa stood up and shook hands with Tucker. He grinned at Caralyn and she hugged him.

"We're going to have meatloaf and cheesy potatoes for dinner. They're Tucker's favorite next to steak and potatoes."

"Mom, do you need any help with dinner?"

"No, Cara. It's almost done. Your father should be home soon."

"If you don't need any help, I'm going home to shower and change clothes."

Tucker was watching TV when she returned. He looked up as she walked into the living room. "Whoa! Look at you. You decided to dress up, huh? What's the occasion. This afternoon you were covered in dirt and dust and smelled like sweat."

She kicked his foot. "I did not smell."

"Of course not. It was someone else."

"Is dinner ready?" Dad asked as he removed his coat and smiled at Caralyn. "What's the occasion? Is it someone's birthday, and I forgot. Happy birthday, Sarah."

"It's not my birthday, and you know it. Let's sit down and eat before things get cold."

"Dinner was delicious, Mom." Caralyn cleared the table and put away the leftovers.

"You could take them home if you want."

"I might if Tucker doesn't eat them later."

"Hey, Cara, do you want to watch a movie or something?" Tucker asked.

"Maybe. Here or at my house?" *You better say at my house, buster.*

"We could try out your TV room. I bet you haven't turned it on since you moved it into your old bedroom."

"Have fun. I will leave the door unlocked," Mom said.

Tucker put his hands on Caralyn's shoulders as they stood on her front porch.

"Did you want to tell me something, Tuck?"

145

"You looked purty in your new dress, Caralyn Ann."

She laughed and poked him in the side. "That's the worst imitation of a hillbilly I ever heard."

"I've been living in Chicago too long."

He followed her inside. She flipped on the lights in the TV room and grabbed the remote.

"What would you like to watch?"

"It doesn't matter, Cara. I just want to spend time with you."

She grinned and chewed her lip.

"Maybe a couple kisses, but no more."

Mom McKay heard Tucker come back shortly after midnight. She smiled and turned over in bed.

"I can make more eggs if you're still hungry."

"Thank, Mom, but I'm stuffed. You make the best omelets in the state."

"If you're going to see Cara before you leave, take the meatloaf and cheesy potatoes to her. She doesn't bother to cook for herself most days. I'm afraid she will wither away to skin and bones."

Tucker knocked on her door and waited outside.

She opened it a moment later wearing her pajamas. "The door's not locked. You could have come in."

"I didn't want to take a chance..."

"Tucker McKay! Were you afraid I would be naked or something?"

He avoided looking at her eyes. "Mom sent over the leftovers. I need to get going. We have a home game tomorrow, and practice later today."

"Do you want to come in for a minute?"

"Yes, but I can't. It was good to see you, Cara. I'll try to be better about calling and staying in touch."

"You better, or else I will come up to the city and get on your case." She set the leftovers on the table by the door and hugged him. "It was good to see you, Bubby."

146

Chapter Twenty-One

"Are you calling because it's April Fool's Day?" Caralyn carried her coffee into the office and booted up her desktop computer.

"No, Cara, I wanted to talk to you. I didn't realize what day it was."

"I remember when I was maybe seven or eight, and you told me a monster was coming to get me unless I played basketball with you."

"You remember that?" He settled into his recliner and grinned.

"I remember. I would have played ball anyway. You didn't have to scare me. I made Grandma look under my bed and in my closet that night."

"I'm sorry I did that, but boys have to tease girls. It's in our DNA."

"Yeah, that's not the only thing in your DNA."

"Did you watch the game last night? Did you see my no-look pass at the end? Alphonse slammed the ball so hard I thought the backboard would never stop shaking."

"It was a good game, and you played the entire fourth quarter."

"Regis was cramping up. I need to pack later. We leave this afternoon for the coast."

"How long will you be gone? Is this the last long road trip of the year?"

"The last one, and I won't be home until a week from next Tuesday."

"At least you guys still have a chance to make the playoffs."

He snorted. "Yeah. Two chances. Slim and none."

"You have a chance until you don't."

"That makes sense."

"I meant until you're mathematically eliminated, dork brain."

"I know what you meant. How's work going? Did you make any money last month? You have bills to pay now that you're a homeowner."

"I had to pays bills when I lived in my apartment. I didn't have to pay all of the rent though."

"You don't have a mortgage. You and Beth own the house outright."

"I still have to pay taxes and utilities. I have to buy groceries and pay the cable bill..."

"Poor baby. Can you hear my tiny violin?"

"Shut up, Tucker."

"Have you finished your book? Would you like me to read it, and give you some feedback? I know a lot about romance novels. I read several each week."

"Make fun of it if you want, but you won't be laughing if a publisher signs me and Hollywood wants to make it into a movie." She watched Mrs. Boyd walking her poodle. "I might have to buy a mansion in Beverly Hills."

"Who do you see playing the leads in the movie?"

She tapped her chin then answered, "I think Katie Williams would be a perfect fit."

"And who would be the husband and the boyfriend?"

"Not you for sure."

"I play ball. I'm not an actor."

"I think I would choose George Downey for the..."

"He's too old. Pick a young actor."

"What about the guy who plays quarterback for the Bears?"

"Steve Wooden? No way! The guy can barely read a defense. No way could he memorize a script."

"Maybe I should play the lead character." She waved at Mrs. Boyd who was now carrying her dog.

"Really? Are you forgetting this is a romance novel. There are several sex scenes. Would you want to do that in a movie?"

"I would if it was done tastefully and essential to the story," she said with a hand in the air. "I am sick of these actresses saying that when they know they would do anything to get a part."

"So you would do a nude scene, huh?"

"If it was done tastefully and essential to the story," she answered then giggled.

"You are a fruitcake, Cara. You could never do it."

"That's why I'm a writer and not an actress. I don't have to think about it."

"Me, too."

She laughed and said, "Like anyone who hire you to play a role in a movie."

"Hey! There have been athletes who make movies."

"And they often win Academy Awards for their skill."

"I'm not saying that, but Michael Jennings did a decent job in *A Basketball Bouncing in the Dirt*."

"That was the exception to the rule, but he was basically playing himself."

Later, Tucker looked at the clock. "Holy cow, Cara! It's almost noon. We've been on the phone for three hours."

"Tell me. I had to put mine on the charger."

"I'm glad we got to talk. I miss our discussions."

"Bull! You miss teasing me, dweeb brain."

"That, too."

"I'll let you go so you can pack. Have a good trip and try to win one or two games. You might still make the playoffs."

"Anything can happen. I'll call when I get settled."

"Would you mind if I go to church with you? You are going, right?" Caralyn asked Mom McKay.

"We are, and you're always welcome to go with us."

"I'll walk over in a few minutes."

"Who was on the phone?" Dad straightened his tie.

Mom walked into the bedroom, checked his tie and adjusted it again. "Caralyn. She wants to go to church with us."

"Really? She hasn't been to our church in quite a while."

"She was going occasionally with Tucker. Maybe that sparked an interest."

149

"Maybe she wants to meet the new preacher. I was talking about him."

"He's single, right?"

Mom walked out of the bedroom. "He is single, but I don't think she's interested in him romantically."

"Are you sure? There aren't many single men in town." He followed her into the kitchen. "She hasn't said it in so many words, but I think she's looking for a husband. She might want to start a family before she's thirty."

Caralyn opened the front door. "I'm here. Are you ready?"

"I need to grab my purse and a jacket, sweetie."

Dad grabbed his coat, wallet and keys and followed her out to the car.

"Is everyone buckled in?" Dad asked looking over his shoulder at Caralyn.

"I am now, Dad." She stared out the window during the short trip to the church.

"It's good to see you Mr. and Mrs. McKay."

"It's good to be here, Pastor Rob. This is Caralyn. She moved back to town from the city a while back."

"Hello, Caralyn. I've heard lots of stories about you. It's a pleasure to finally meet you."

"It's good to meet you, too, Pastor Lucas." She smiled at him. *You're sure a lot younger than Pastor Grissom, and I hear you're single. I might like to get to know you better.*

"Please call me Rob. I'm rather informal." He smiled at Caralyn and watched her walk away before turning his attention to the next person entering the church.

She smiled back and followed the McKays to a pew.

"That was a good message, Pastor Lucas."

"Thank you, Mr. McKay." He shook his hand. "I hope I didn't ruffle too many feathers. I know Pastor Grissom was here for many years and rather set in his ways. I hope the church is ready for fresh ideas."

"I think fresh ideas are exactly what this church needs."

Caralyn smiled as Pastor Lucas shook her hand. "I hope to see you again, Caralyn."

"I think it could be arranged." She cringed as she walked to the car. *Shoot! I hope he doesn't think I was flirting too much. I was kinda flirting, but I don't want him to get the wrong idea about me.*

"Is there some reason you made the trip home?" Caralyn asked while frosting a cake. "Not that I don't like seeing you, but Mom said something about a special occasion." She giggled and asked, "Would you have any idea what she meant? I don't think it's a holiday."

Tucker walked up behind her, put one hand on her back and used a finger of the other one to swipe some of the frosting.

"Stop that! You'll mess it up."

"Hmmm. Tastes pretty good. Did you make it from scratch, or is it from a can?"

She turned around and poked his stomach with the spatula. "It's from a box, but I might not let you have any unless you're nice to me."

"Why would I be nice to you? You haven't called me all week."

"I texted you and asked what you would like for dinner tonight. Doesn't that count?"

"I suppose. Do I have time to run home, shower and talk to Mom and Dad before dinner?"

"Dinner won't be ready for a half hour. Mom made a salad to go along with the lasagna. I hope it turns out okay."

"The salad or the lasagna?" he asked with a grin.

"The lasagna, you dweeb. Mom knows how to make a salad, but I'm not sure how the lasagna will turn out. I haven't made it very often."

"I'm sure it will be fine. I'll be back soon." He hesitated but then kissed her cheek. "You smell good, Carrie."

"I probably smell like pasta sauce."

"I might decide to... never mind."

"Tell Mom I have French, ranch and thousand island dressing here."

"Should I save room for cake after dinner?" He tried to swipe more frosting, but she pushed his hand away.

"Go shower and you better behave after dinner."

"Can I help with anything, Cara?"

"I've got everything ready, Mom. The table is set and the lasagna is ready. I made green beans with onions and bacon. What would you like to drink?"

"Water is okay for us. Tucker is ready, but Derren called. He'll be here after they get through talking."

"Did she file for the divorce?"

"I believe so, and he's not going to contest it. She doesn't want anything from him."

"What about the house?"

"Derren offered to buy her half of it."

"He should move back here. He could get a job teaching and coaching in Butler if Stockton Woods doesn't have an opening."

"He probably makes quite a bit more in West Memphis."

Tucker walked in a few minutes later.

"Now that the birthday boy has arrived, we are ready to eat," Caralyn said with a grin.

"Are we going to sing now or when we have cake?" Dad asked.

"Later," Mom replied.

"I will say the prayer."

"Okay, Tucker. Go ahead."

"Wow! The lasagna turned out all right. I wasn't sure if I added enough rat poison."

Dad coughed and looked at Caralyn.

"I only added it to Tucker's side of the pan, Daddy."

After clearing the table and putting away the leftovers, Caralyn set the cake on the dining room table.

"I didn't want to burn down the house, so I bought a two and a five." Caralyn lit the candles and waited.

"Does it mean I'm fifty-two?"

"Ooops!" Caralyn switched the candles. "There. Twenty-five going on twelve. Blow them out after you make a wish."

"I know the routine." He grinned at her then blew the candles out with a mighty blast.

"You didn't have to blow the candles off the cake, dweeb brain."

"I'll cut the cake. Cara, do you have any ice cream?" Mom asked.

"I'll get it. I have vanilla and chocolate."

"I'll take some of each."

"I knew you'd say that, Daddy. Tucker, what would you like?"

"I'll just have cake for now." He rubbed his stomach. "I might have room for ice cream later."

After eating the desert, Caralyn brought out a gift and handed it to Tucker. "I couldn't think of anything nice to get you, so I bought this."

He smiled and ripped off the paper. "Where did you find wrapping paper with footballs on it?"

"In the kids' section of Topps Discount in Butler."

"You do realize I play basketball, right?"

Caralyn sighed and said, "I couldn't remember. I knew it was some game for adolescents."

He opened the box and grinned. "Where did you find this?"

"The bookstore in Mount Trenton had it in stock. No! It was in the bargain bin. It was marked down to a buck."

"I know it wasn't. Thanks, Cara. I'll read it tonight. Coach Wooden has always been an inspiration."

"You might not have time to read it tonight," Mom said after catching the look on Caralyn's face. "You could read it when you get back to the city."

He looked at Mom then Caralyn. "Yeah. I can wait.

"Dinner was excellent, Cara. Thank you." Dad hugged her.

153

Mom hugged Caralyn and whispered, "Tucker might not tell you, but he loved your dinner."

"I know. He ate enough to feed an army."

"I'll leave the back door unlocked in case he comes home late. I don't know if he has his key."

"He can crash here if he stays real late. I have an extra bedroom, Mom."

"What do you want to do, Cara?" Tucker asked. "We could go out or stay here and watch a movie or something."

"Since it's started to rain, would you mind if we don't go out?"

"I don't mind." He entered the TV room and found the remote. "We could watch baseball or basketball. Do you have a preference?" Tucker asked flipping through the channels.

She joined him on the couch. "I only watch baseball if I need help falling asleep. Who's playing basketball tonight?"

"The Lakers are playing the Jazz."

She shrugged. "Not really interested. How about a movie?"

"On TV or a DVD?"

"I don't have any new DVDs, and we've watched all the ones I have." She looked at Tucker and bit her lip. "Maybe we could talk."

"Sure. Should we talk about the weather? Or your books? What's on your mind?"

"Religion." She sat against the arm of the couch and put her feet against his thigh.

"Okay. What about it?"

"I met the new pastor. He's about my age and he's single."

Tucker grinned at her. "Did you ask him out?"

She kicked him. "No, but I would go out if he asked."

"Was he the only reason you went to church?" Tucker grabbed her foot and began massaging it.

"Not the only reason. I know you've changed since you started going to Pastor Duncan's church. I know there's a difference between his church and ours here in town."

154

"There is a difference between the Nazarene denomination and the Methodists, but there are many similarities."

They talked about church, religion and spirituality for the next hour.

Tucker noticed her yawning and got up. "I should head home. You're falling asleep."

She stood up and faced him. She looked up and said, "You don't have to go. You could stay here. You can use the spare bedroom if you want."

He knew what she was really asking. "Cara, I shouldn't. It wouldn't look right."

"Why not?"

"Because it's not the proper thing to do."

She pushed him away. "I'm not saying you have to sleep in my bed, creepo. I have a guest bedroom."

"I wasn't considering sleeping with you, Caralyn. That would be a sin, and don't you dare say..."

"I wasn't going to say it's all right because we've done it before. I'm not stupid." She wiped away some tears. "I've been feeling I need God in my life like He's in yours, but I don't know what to do. I know I have to say a prayer, but..."

He pulled her into his arms and whispered, "Just tell God you need Him and that you repent of your sins."

"All of them? Do I have to mention every one? I can't remember every bad thing I've done."

"I don't think you have to make a list. Just that you repent of all of them."

She rested her face on his chest and prayed.

"Is that all there is to it?" She dried her eyes.

"It is as long as you are sincere."

"I think I am."

Chapter Twenty-Two

"Now I have time to talk to you, Caralyn. Thanks for waiting."

"No problem, Pastor Rob."

"I heard Tucker was home for a couple days."

Caralyn watched as the church emptied. "He came home for his birthday, and I made dinner for us."

"He texted me and said you made a profession of faith."

"I did. I know Tucker's life has changed because of the church he attends." She waved her hands. "That's not exactly what I meant. I know it has nothing to do with the church building or even the people. He has a relationship with Jesus and that's what I want."

"I can help if you have any questions."

"Thank you, Pastor Rob."

"You are welcome. I didn't see your... the McKays today. Are they out of town?"

"They went to Kentucky for the weekend. They are thinking of buying a vacation home." She grinned and said, "You were going to call them my parents, weren't you?"

"Yes, I admit I think of you as their daughter. I know most of the story, but not everything."

"Perhaps I could tell you more over dinner sometime."

He smiled. "Is that an official dinner invitation?"

"I suppose it is. You are allowed to have dinner with people in the church, right?"

"I am, and there's more."

"What?"

"As a single man, I am even allowed to date eligible females even if they are as pretty as you."

She blushed and chewed her lip for a moment. "Do you have plans for Tuesday evening?"

"If I do, I could use an excuse to get out of them."

"I don't want to cause an issue. I could make dinner another night."

"Not necessary. I know I don't have anything on the schedule for Tuesday. If the offer stands, I would love to have dinner with you."

"I can put together a mean meatloaf and scrumptious cheesy potatoes."

"Sounds delicious. What time works for you?"

"Is six too early?"

He shook his head. "I often eat early. Can I bring anything?"

"Just an appetite."

"Then I will carve it in stone on my schedule," he said with a smile. "I will see you then."

"You can call me if something comes up and you need to cancel. Preachers are like doctors. You are on call 24/7."

"Maybe, but I can screen my calls if I want."

"I talked to Pastor Rob after church today, Tuck. I told him about the other night."

"How did he react?" Tucker asked as he turned off the TV.

"He was pleased and offered to help with any questions I have."

"When I talked to him, I got the feeling he was a good guy. He is single, too, if that makes a difference."

"Yes, and I kinda invited him for dinner Tuesday."

"Really?"

Caralyn waited for him to elaborate.

"Are you still there, Tuck?"

"I'm here."

"Are you mad because I invited him for dinner?" She twisted her hair around a finger. "It's just dinner. He is interested in my past."

"Your past?" he asked slowly. "Really?"

"My family history, you goof. He thinks of Mom and Dad as my parents, but he knows they aren't my birth parents."

"I'm not mad about you making dinner for him as long as... never mind."

"As long as what, Tuck? Tell me." She let go of her hair. "I want to know what's on your mind."

"Is it a date?"

"It's dinner with the pastor of my church."

"You're evading the question, Cara. I bet he thinks it's a date."

"I haven't flirted with him, but he did say I was pretty."

Tucker laughed. "He might need glasses."

She stuck her tongue out at the phone.

"Did you just stick your tongue out at me, young lady?"

"You better believe it, dweeb breath. Don't you think I'm pretty? Does that make me sound vain?"

"A little."

"A little what? Pretty, or vain?"

"You know I think you're pretty. Only you know if you're vain."

She twisted her hair around a finger again. "Maybe a little, but I don't look in the mirror all day."

"If you were vain, you wouldn't act like a tomboy."

"I don't act like a tomboy anymore. I did when I was a kid, but not now."

"Have Mom and Dad returned?"

"Not yet. I don't expect them home until after dark. Do you think they will buy a vacation home?"

He shrugged. "They might. They have talked about it for years. If they find a place they like, they might pull the trigger. They have the money."

"I could..."

Tucker waved a finger. "Don't even suggest it. They will never take your money."

"They never used any of it after Grandma passed away. They could have because I was living with them."

"And Pastor Rob probably heard that and is confused about everything."

"It is difficult to explain our relationship to people outside of Stockton Woods."

"I think it's just the opposite. People who don't live in town, don't know us. They don't think we're related like people in town."

"Whatever. I'm going to make meatloaf and cheesy potatoes."

"Good choice. You won't poison him..."

"You're a dweeb. I'll call you later and let you know how it goes."

"I don't want to know if he kisses you."

"I don't plan to let him kiss me."

"But he might have designs on you."

She shook her head. "He's a preacher. He has to be a gentleman."

"I heard the car," Caralyn followed Mom into the house. "How was your weekend? Did you find a place you like?"

"We did, and we put a deposit on it."

"Tell me all about it. Is it on a lake like Dad wanted?"

Dad walked in with the suitcases. "Did you hear about the vacation property we bought?"

"Mom was telling me. Are you happy with it?"

Dad carried the suitcases into the bedroom and Caralyn followed.

"The only negative thing is it doesn't have a fireplace. It's similar to the cabin we rented a few years ago. It has a big back porch and there is a hot tub, but it's not on the porch."

Caralyn sat on the edge of the bed. "I hope you get to use it often enough to make it worthwhile."

Mom opened her suitcase and began to unpack. "Since we are teachers with summers off, we can use it then, but it's close enough to use during long weekends or week long breaks."

"You will retire at some point. Do you think you might live there full-time?"

Mom grinned and answered, "That might depend on if we have grandchildren somewhere."

Dad froze at the mention of grandchildren.

Caralyn checked the living room, looking in the mirror and adjusted her hair. Then she opened the door.

"Good evening, Caralyn. I hope I'm not too early."

"You're right on time. Come in, Pastor Rob." She held the door for him.

"Thank you, but please call me Rob." He looked around. "I know you remodeled and built an addition, but you have retained the charm of an older home."

"I wanted to retain as much of the old house as I could but still update it for the future. Would you like a tour? Dinner is ten minutes from being ready."

"Yes, I would like the complete tour, please," he said with a grin.

"Let's go this way first. This is where the addition starts..."

They heard the timer go off as she brought him into the kitchen.

"We timed that right."

"It smells delicious, Caralyn. My mother used to make meatloaf for my father, but she doesn't cook much now."

"Why not?"

"They live in an assisted living facility in Florida. The meals are provided."

"Are your parents retired? I wouldn't have thought they were old enough." Caralyn took the meatloaf and potatoes out of the oven and turned it off. "I think dinner is ready."

"I'm the youngest of five siblings. My parents are in their mid-sixties. I was born when my mother turned forty."

"I'm ready to eat if you are. We can fill our plates and sit at the kitchen table. It's less formal."

After saying a prayer, Rob asked, "I know the McKays are not your birth parents, but I don't know what happened to your... how do you refer to them?"

"The Dawsons, Barbara and Douglas, are my birth parents. The McKays are my parents. I've always called them Mom and Dad."

She explained how and where the accident happened and growing up with Grandma Florence and the McKays."

"I can understand why you and Tucker are so close. You really did grow up together." He took another bite. "The meat loaf is delicious. Is it a family recipe?"

"It's either Mom's or Grandma's. Grandma Stanfield. Grandma Florence was never a great cook. I learned how to cook with Grandma's help on the farm."

"If you don't mind me asking, why didn't the McKays adopt you after your grandmother passed away?"

"They were my guardians, but never formally adopted me. I never thought it was necessary."

"Did you ever live with your sister?"

"I would spend time in the city during the summer and occasionally during holidays, but not full-time." She saw his plate was empty. "There is more. Help yourself."

He filled his plate again. "You have a masters degree, but you don't have a full-time job, do you?"

"Not yet." She got more food and sat down. "I tried to find one with one of the large publishing companies in the city, but all they would offer was secretarial work." She added ketchup to her meatloaf. "That's not what I wanted."

"How can you afford this house and pay your bills? Sorry, I'm being nosy."

She waved a hand. "It's okay. It's not a secret in Stockton Woods that Beth and I got a large sum of money from the trucking company after the accident. It was put into a trust. I'm old enough now to draw some of the money. I only take what I need, and I earn a little from editing jobs. I made a thousand dollars last week doing translating work for a Chicago company. I'm not bragging, but I can speak and write in four languages. Grandma taught French, so I grew up bilingual. I picked up Spanish and Italian during my semester in France. I kinda have a knack for languages."

"I had trouble learning English," he teased.

After clearing the dishes, they moved to the TV room and sat at opposite ends of the couch.

"What do you like best about Stockton Woods, Rob?"

"I like the people..."

As they talked, Caralyn's thoughts were of Tucker. *I like Rob, and he's interesting, but I'd rather be here with Tucker if I'm being honest.* She laughed at his joke about preachers and rabbis. *Rob is funny, good-looking and would be a catch for any girl, but he doesn't have the chemistry I feel with Tucker.*

"Would you let me read your book when it's finished?"

"Does that mean you wouldn't buy a copy? Should the church increase your salary?"

He smiled. "Would you sign it if I buy it?"

"Maybe."

"I know better than to ask ladies at the church how old they are, but I'm confused. Tucker is almost three years older than you, but you graduated from high school only a year behind him. How did that happen?"

"My birthday is at the end of November, and that was the cutoff date at the time. I started school when I was four. A year later I skipped first grade." She shrugged and said, "That's how it happened. I was always a year or more younger than my classmates, so I got used to dealing with older kids."

"How old are you now?"

"Seventeen. How old do I look?"

He stared at her, but she kept a straight face.

"Okay. I know you aren't seventeen, but..."

"I'm twenty-two. I earned my master's degree last August, and have been job hunting while working on my book since then. How old are you?"

I was born on June 2, 1985, so that makes me... let me do the math." He used his fingers to count. "I will be twenty-six on my birthday."

She looked at a photo of Tucker on the wall. "You are a year and a couple months older than Tucker, but he acts like a high school kid. He's so immature. His job is to play a game kids play."

162

"I've seen him play ball. The town must be pretty proud of him."

She rolled her eyes. "They wanted to name the gym after him, but saner minds prevailed."

"I tried out for the basketball team, but I got cut. I did play baseball, but I was always a reserve."

"Not many of the girls in high school were into sports, but we did have a basketball team, volleyball and softball. I played on all three and was a cheerleader, too. I did okay in softball and basketball because I always played with the boys, but I sucked at volleyball. I only made the team because we needed bodies."

"I would challenge you to a game of tennis, but you'd probably beat me."

"I've always been competitive in whatever I do. I hate to lose, or do worse than my best."

"Does that apply to your writing?"

"They don't keep score, but I have to challenge myself."

He checked the time and stood up. "I should go. I do have to return a couple calls and start preparing for Sunday."

"I hope my meatloaf didn't poison you." She followed him to the door and out onto the porch. *Should I let him kiss me? Pastors are like other men. They have certain needs and desires.* She took a deep breath. *I won't make the first move, but I will let him kiss me if he wants. If I like it, I will kiss him back.*

Rob looked up at the sky then back at Caralyn.

What is he going to do? I would kinda like to know if he has any feelings toward me.

"I like how you can see the stars even in town," Rob said.

That was dorky, but he must be kinda nervous. I should say something to ease the tension, but he still has to make the first move. "I should practice my serve in case we ever play tennis. I wouldn't want to let you win." *Crap! That was just as dorky.*

"We will have to make time for it, Ms. Dawson."

He smiled and left without giving her a kiss, hug or even a handshake."

"How did your dinner with Pastor Rob go?" Mom asked the next evening. "Did you learn much about him?"

Caralyn sat at the kitchen table. "We learned quite a bit about each other, but I have to admit I was thinking about Tucker most of the night. Rob's a good guy, but he's not Tucker. It was awkward when he left, but I'll tell you later."

Mom sat across from Caralyn and looked into her eyes. "You can't hide your feelings for him from me. I'm your mother."

Caralyn laughed. "You're Tucker's mother, too. That makes it kinda weird."

"I know he *talks* to Nancy when he stops by the cemetery maybe you should have a *talk* with her."

"I might visit the cemetery after church. I haven't been there for a while."

"You told me what Nancy wanted you and Tucker to do after she was gone."

"Yes, but maybe it's too soon. She hasn't been gone for a year."

"It's been eleven months and Nancy didn't want Tucker to wait long before... you know."

"He has been calling or texting almost every day. I miss him if I don't talk to him."

"I think he feels the same, sweetie." Mom patted Caralyn's hand. "It's a unique situation, but you can't worry about what people might think. You and Tucker love each other. You always have."

"I suppose that's why it's never worked out for me to be in a relationship with anyone else."

"Mom, I'm going to the cemetery."

"Okay, sweetie." Mom nodded as they left the church. "Should I save you something for lunch? Jim and I are going to see Grandma and Grandpa."

"I'll grab something from The Curve."

"Open your heart, Cara. You will do the right thing."

Caralyn drove to the Lincoln Ridge Cemetery and walked past her parents' and grandparents' graves. She thought about them for a moment before approaching Nancy's gravesite. She cleaned up the area and then sat in front of the granite headstone. She closed her eyes and thought about Nancy's last request.

"What should I do, Nancy? You were right about so many things. I do love him, and he loves me. It did hurt when he married you, but you needed him. You told him not to wait too long, but I wish I knew if it's too soon for us to think about being together." She closed her eyes, sighed and sat quietly. After a moment she opened her eyes and laughed. "Why is there always a train going by when I visit the cemetery?" She heard the distinct sound of a train, but when she looked at the tracks, there wasn't one in sight. She felt the wind rustle through the trees and saw two small clouds merge into one. "Is that your sign, Nancy?" she asked as tears flooded her eyes. She dried her eyes and saw her first two robins of the spring fly from one tree to another.

Chapter Twenty-Three

"Pastor Duncan, I need to talk to you. When would you be available?" Tucker asked.

"I don't have plans for lunch. Would now work for you?"

"I don't want to take you away from your family."

Pastor Duncan dismissed the thought with a wave. "Renae is taking the kids to see her parents in Michigan. I'm all alone for a couple days."

"I'll buy if we stop somewhere."

"Deal." Pastor Duncan shook Tucker's hand. "Give me ten minutes to get ready."

"I'll drive and bring you back if that's okay."

"Sounds good.

"This is the place we ate lunch with Quinn and Claire." Tucker parked the Jeep and they headed inside. The hostess seated them and they decided on burgers and fries.

When the waitress walked away after taking their orders, Pastor Duncan said, "I have an idea what might be on your mind, but I will let you tell me in case I am wrong."

"It's Caralyn." Tucker turned the ketchup bottle upside down and slumped his shoulders.

"I thought that might be the case. What concerns you?"

"I love her, and I'm pretty sure she loves me. Nancy hasn't been gone for a year, but she told me not to wait too long before I... you know."

"Some people grieve for much longer than others. I don't know of any hard and fast rule that says you have to wait for a specific length of time before moving on. You can still love Nancy and her memory if you resume your life."

"I kinda understand that, but I was wondering if people will think a relationship with Caralyn might not be..." He paused and looked out the window.

"Unique?"

"That's for sure."

"Caralyn might have grown up with your family, but she is not technically related to you by blood. She would not even be considered a stepsister really."

"I think about how she calls my parents Mom and Dad and wonder if people will be confused."

Pastor Duncan chuckled. "I admit it did give me pause at first."

"I guess I'm asking for the okay to go ahead and ask her to marry me."

"Have you thought about where you will live. She moved back to Stockton Woods, right?"

"Yes, and I need to live in Chicagoland as long as I'm playing for the Bulls. I suppose we could have a place in the city and one back home."

"Will you live in Stockton Woods after your career?"

"If not in the town, at least somewhere close. I could see us buying a place in the country. She's always loved the farm."

"You mentioned going into coaching. Is that still your goal?"

"Yes, it is." Tucker smiled as the waitress brought their food.

Pastor Duncan prayed and said, "I can never eat all the fries, but I try."

"Thanks for hearing me out, Pastor Aaron. I don't have any doubts about Caralyn now."

"I am always available if you need to talk." He shook hands with Tucker as they got ready to leave."

"I appreciate that."

They walked out and got into Tucker's Jeep.

"Have the Bulls been eliminated from the playoffs? I admit I don't follow professional sports too closely."

"Unfortunately, we have. Some fans might think we should lose the rest of our games to get a better position in the draft, but we still play to win every game."

167

"Where are you?" Caralyn asked.

"In the Jeep on my way home. I have the day off and thought I would drive down to see Mom and Dad. What are you doing?"

"Going through my email and Facebook posts. Do you think you might have time to see me for a few minutes while you're here?"

"Uh, maybe a minute or two," he teased.

"You're such a dweeb. Should I make you something special for dinner?"

"Whatever you want. I'm not picky." He passed a row of trucks on the Interstate and changed the channel on the radio.

"I have some old bologna I could fry and a few moldy slices of bread."

"Do you have pickles and mustard?"

"I think so. Why?"

"Don't you remember how we would make mustard and pickle sandwiches when we were kids?"

"I remember. Didn't we add potato chips at times?"

"Yeah. Could you make a couple of those for dinner?"

"I'll see if I still have the recipe," she replied with a giggle.

Tucker arrived before lunch. He parked the Jeep and headed next door to see Caralyn since the McKays were still in school.

"That didn't take long. What time did you leave?"

"Around seven thirty. Are my sandwiches ready?" He grinned and poked her ribs.

"I couldn't find the recipe, so I'll have to wing it. I'm not sure I have bread and butter pickles."

"Is that what we used to use?" Tucker asked as he sat at the kitchen table.

"That's what Grandma calls them. She used to preserve them in those mason jars."

"I bet she still has some in the cellar."

After lunch they drove to Uncle Alton's lake.

"I can't believe we used to swim in the lake and Grandpa's pond. I don't think I would like swimming here now. The water's kinda dark."

"It was always like that, Cara."

They sat on the edge of the dock. She took off her shoes and socks and could barely reach the water.

"Do you think the Bulls will fire Coach Halas since the team sucks this year? The owners should fire the players, but it's easier to change coaches."

He shrugged. "The players like him, but that might not be a good thing. Sometimes I felt he should have been tougher on us."

"It can't be easy because the players make so much more money then he does. Don't tell them I said so, but there are a couple players on your team who only care about their stats. They must have performance bonuses in their contracts."

"It's the coach's responsibility to get all the players to work together as a team. As one unit. The NBA is different than college ball. It's a lot more one on one or three on three. Teams don't play defense the whole game. They pick their spots."

"I watched a game between you guys and the Celtics. You had a big lead and blew it because Joel Isaiah couldn't guard a statue."

"He's not the best defensive player on the team."

Caralyn snorted. "Ha! He is lazy and complains every time he gets a foul called on him. On offense he whines if the defense touches him. He's a big baby. Management should trade him for a pair of old sneakers. With or without laces. Doesn't matter."

"You should be in charge of personnel, Cara."

She bumped his shoulder and made a face. He put an arm around her and held her close. They looked at each other for a moment.

"Are you going to kiss me, Tucker?" she whispered. *Please say yes!*

"Would you mind if I did?"

"Did you brush your teeth after lunch? You might taste like pickles..."

He took her in his arms and kissed her. He pulled her onto his lap and kissed her several more times.

"Do I taste like pickles?"

"Maybe, but I still like your kisses."

She shifted her position and lost her balance. Tucker tried to catch her, but she fell into the water.

"Are you okay, Carrie?" He grabbed her hand and laughed while pulling her back onto the dock. "It's a good thing the water's only a few feet deep by the dock. You would have gotten soaked."

"Most of me is wet, you goofus."

"At least it's kinda hot today. You won't freeze."

"The sun will dry my clothes."

Tucker got ready to leave after having dinner with his parents and Caralyn.

"Thanks for coming to see us." Mom leaned close and whispered, "I know you came home to see Caralyn, but we like to see you, too."

"I might not make it back before the end of the season. We have one more long road trip and the last couple games are at home. I'll head down as soon as I can."

"Drive safely, and don't get hurt."

"I'll walk you out to the car," Caralyn said.

"Could you carry my bag, please?"

She poked his arm. "You can carry your own stuff."

"Should I carry you? I used to when you were a kid." He set his bag on the ground and picked her up. "You've gained a couple pounds over the years."

"Shut up and set me down."

He set her down and she stuck out her tongue. "You're a creepo, buster."

"And you are a delinquent."

She put her arms around his neck and he pulled her close and kissed her.

"I suppose I will have to get used to that, huh?" Dad McKay whispered as he put an arm around his wife's waist.

"They are more demonstrative than Nancy was with Tucker."

Caralyn sat in the kitchen and talked on the phone to Tucker while Mom made dinner and listened. She picked at the small scar on her knee and laughed.

"Why should I say I love you? You missed two free throws last night. I could make them with my eyes closed."

"Did you see why I was shooting free throws?" Tucker asked.

"I saw number fifteen from the Bucks bump you as you tried to dunk the ball." She giggled and grinned at Mom.

"A slight bump, huh?" Tucker asked. "He hit me so hard I landed ten feet out of bounds."

"Poor baby. Did you fall down and bump your knee?' Do you want me to kiss it and put a Superman Bandaid on it?"

Mom shook her head as she listened to the kids teasing each other.

"Did you do anything productive today, or were you lazy?"

"I wrote another chapter to my book, and did some editing on Sharon Foggett's project. I did laundry and cleaned both bathrooms."

"Sounds like you've become a real Suzy Homemaker."

"At least I didn't have to hire someone to clean my house."

Tucker rolled his eyes. "I hired a company because I often have to be gone for a week or two at a time. They do more than dust and check the mail."

"Whatever. Are you going to call me before you leave for San Antonio?"

"Maybe."

"You better call me, Tucker McKay."

Dad entered the kitchen, checked the stove and looked at Caralyn sitting on the table with her feet on the chair. "Are they bickering?"

Mom shook her head. "They are teasing each other like they were still kids."

171

"He called her earlier. How often do they talk to each other?" He sniffed the pasta and looked in the oven at the garlic bread. "Are we having salad, too?"

"They call each other every hour," Mom said.

Caralyn looked at her parents and shook her head. "We only talk a few times a day."

Dad took a deep breath. "He is coming home when the season ends, right?"

"Yes."

"They will be all over each other."

"Daddy! How can you say that? We aren't... never mind. What did you say, Tuck? I was talking to Mom and Dad."

"I asked if you wanted to come up for the last two home games. Do you?"

"Why? You guys will lose."

For the next two weeks, Tucker and Caralyn talked for two or three hours a day. Sometimes he would call in the middle of the night from the hotel after a game. The basketball season ended on May twenty-sixth with another loss. Tucker cleaned out his locker at the practice facility, talked to Coach Halas and rushed back to his apartment. He hurriedly packed enough clothes for a couple weeks. He checked the apartment one last time, called the company who cleaned his apartment and told them he would be gone for two weeks or more. He loaded the Jeep, turned on some music and headed out of the city.

As he approached New Lebanon he checked the time. *Should I stop at Nico's and grab some sandwiches, or should I not bother?* He decided to keep going. *Caralyn won't mind if I don't stop.*

He made it home in less time than normal. He threw the Jeep in park, grabbed his large duffel bag and ran into the house.

"Hi, Dad. How are you? Where's Mom? I can't stay. I need to see Caralyn." He dashed into his bedroom, threw the duffel bag on the bed and raced into the kitchen. "Hi, Mom. I thought you might still be at school."

"We had a half day today. Where are you rushing off to?"

"I need to talk to Caralyn. Is she home?" He didn't wait for an answer. He sped through the kitchen and utility room, jumped down the steps and sprinted across the yard. He took the back steps three at a time and walked into Caralyn's kitchen. "It's me. Where are you?"

"In my office. What do you want? I'm busy working. I'm trying to translate French into Italian for someone at the airport in St. Louis."

He took a deep breath, felt the small box in his pocket and tried to calm his heart as he walked through the kitchen, dining room, across the hall and into her office.

She held up a finger as she spoke rapidly into her phone. She ended the call and sighed. "I had to try to calm down a grandmother trying to locate her two grandchildren. I didn't expect you this early."

"I made good time."

"Does that mean you didn't stop at Nico's?"

"I thought about it, but decided it was more important to get home as fast as possible."

She shrugged and stood up. "Why? Do you have a hot date?"

He pulled out the small box. "Kinda." He put his hands on her shoulders. "Caralyn Ann Dawson, will you marry me sometime this summer if you aren't too busy? Mom and Dad said it was okay. They kinda want me out of the house."

She stared at him like he had suddenly gone insane.

"What? Is this a flashback to the night you proposed to Nancy?"

"I'd like to marry you if you don't mind. Not today, but sometime soon. What do you say? Do you want to get hitched?"

"If you are teasing me, I am going to murder you until you are stone cold dead, but if you are serious, then my answer is yes. Which is it?"

He moved her hands around his neck, put his arms around her, pulled her close and kissed her deeply.

173

This better not be a dream. She kissed him with more passion.

He broke off the kiss and asked, "Did you answer? I wasn't listening."

"You are absolutely terrible at making proposals, but I will marry you, Tucker McKay." She locked her lips onto his and didn't let go until she needed to breathe.

"You said yes, right?"

"Yes, you twerp! I said yes." She kissed him again.

"Good. I was hoping you'd agree. I bought this ring. I hope you like it."

"Are you going to open the box and let me see it? That might be a good idea, twerp brain."

"Yeah, right." He opened it and handed the box to her. "You can try it on if you want. I think I got the right size."

"No way! You need to put it on my finger."

He placed the ring on her finger and she admired it.

"Does it fit okay?"

"Perfectly."

"Good. Should we tell Mom and Dad, or should we call them?"

She shook her head, laughed and answered, "I think we could walk next door and tell them in person. You are such a lovable goof."

"Should I carry you over my shoulder?"

"No, I think I can walk." *Actually, I might float next door. I am so happy I might burst.*

He held her hand as they walked across the yard and into the utility room.

"We're back," Tucker hollered. "We have something to tell you."

"We are in the living room," Mom responded looking at her husband. "Do you think it's what I thought it might be?"

"Who knows? He might want to tell us they're going to play ball in the backyard."

Mom shook her head.

Dad laughed.

"I think I should carry you to the living room, Carrie." He picked her up, kissed her and tried to fit through the doorway.

"You never learn, Tucker. Turn sideways."

He managed to get through both doorways.

"What's going on?" Dad asked. "Did Cara hurt something? Why are you carrying her?"

"Put me down, Tuck," she said softly.

He set her down in front of the couch and stood behind her with his hands on her shoulders.

She grinned and held out her hand.

Mom gasped and put a hand to her mouth.

Dad stared at the ring.

Tucker smiled.

"Tucker asked me to marry him, and for some reason, I said yes."

"Oh, sweetie." Mom jumped up and hugged Caralyn. "I am so happy for you. Both of you." She hugged and kissed her son.

Dad stood up, scratched his ear and shook Tucker's hand.

Tucker hugged his father.

"Does this mean you're my son and my son-in-law, too?"

"Oh, Daddy!" Caralyn said letting him see the ring before she hugged him and put her head on his chest.

Tucker scratched his jaw. "I don't know how to answer that. It's kinda weird not to have in-laws, or to have the in-laws be the same for both the bride and groom."

"It took some time accepting how you feel about each other," Dad said as he squeezed Caralyn.

Caralyn grinned and said, "Think how weird it would be if you had formally adopted me."

Chapter Twenty-Four

"I can make us some tea, and we can talk about the wedding."

"Okay, but I don't want to wait too long, Mom."

"But this is your wedding, sweetie. Don't you want to walk down the aisle in your wedding gown and have a big reception?" Mom poured water into the coffee maker and picked out a peach-flavored tea.

"I used to dream about that, but not anymore. I'd rather have a small wedding so we can get married without a long wait."

Mom looked at her.

Caralyn waved a hand. "Not just because I don't want to wait to have sex, but... I don't know. I would rather have a simple wedding with you, Dad and maybe a couple family members in attendance."

"I admit I am a little surprised you have waited to..."

"We talked about it and decided it would be what God wants us to do." She grinned and said, "We have done some stuff."

Mom turned away. "I don't need to know, and neither does your father."

"Hi, Daddy. How are you today?"

He kissed the top of her head then kissed his wife.

"We've been talking about the wedding."

"I heard."

"Did you hear the part about not having sex?" Caralyn asked.

"Yes. How does Tucker feel about it?"

"Daddy!"

"No, not the sex part. The idea of a simple wedding. Have you talked to him about what he wants?"

"Of course, and he said it would be my decision."

"He probably doesn't want to wait too long either." Dad sat next to Caralyn. "Not that he said anything."

"Who said anything?" Tucker walked into the kitchen, opened the fridge and looked for a bottle of water.

"We're talking about the wedding. I told Mom I don't want to wait, and she thinks it's because I'm horny and want to have sex right away. Sex as a married woman, I mean."

Tucker looked at Caralyn, then Mom and lastly at his father. "I'm ready to head out to the farm if you are."

Dad stood up. "Yep! Let's go. The women can talk all they want about the wedding and other stuff."

Caralyn giggled and whispered, "Men are so easy to embarrass." She stood up and kissed Tucker. "What are you going to do at the farm?"

"Grandpa needs someone to fix a couple places in the fence around the chicken house."

"Have fun. I'll be waiting when you get back." Caralyn kissed him again and swatted his butt.

They waited until the men left. Caralyn sat back down, put her elbows on the table and her chin in her hands and sighed.

"What is it, Cara.?"

"I need to talk to you about what Nancy told us, and me privately, about what she wanted after she was gone."

Mom poured them each a cup of tea. "Go ahead."

"She knew she didn't have long to wait, so she told us not to spend a long time grieving. She actually told us to get married and have the family she wanted. We tried to tell her she would get better, but she knew the truth. She was in a lot of pain in spite of the meds. She kinda made a joke about Tucker starving because he couldn't boil water."

Mom laughed. "He's better now."

"Later, when I was alone with her, she told me she knew I still loved him and was sorry for taking him away. She said God knew she would only be here a little while. Now I kinda understand what she meant."

"Do you worry about Tucker still loving Nancy?"

Caralyn shook her head emphatically. "Not in the least. I want him to always love her. I love her. I don't want us to ever forget her and how she and Tucker loved each other."

"Mom, I'm taking Caralyn to the cemetery this morning. It's the first anniversary of... you know."

"I understand. We will visit the cemetery later." She patted his hand.

He walked across the yard and into Caralyn's kitchen. He saw her standing at the sink doing dishes. He walked up behind her, put his arms around her from behind and kissed her neck.

"I don't know who's doing that, but you will need to stop before my fiancee gets here."

"Do you often let strange men into your house and let them kiss you and touch you here?"

"Not often, but occasionally. If you keep touching me there, we won't be able to wait until after the wedding. You will have to carry me to my bed and ravage my body all morning."

"Is that what happens in your romance novel? Does the male lead *ravage* the damsel in distress?"

"Do you even know what that word means, Tucker?"

"Maybe not exactly, but I know it has something to do with sex." He lightly massaged her bottom and stepped back.

She faced him, grinned and said, "'I knew it was you."

"That's a relief."

"Either you or Davey or Richard or..."

"You've made your point, delinquent."

"I'll be ready to leave in a couple minutes. Do I look okay?"

Tucker chuckled. "I don't think it matters, Carrie."

"I know Nancy can't see me, you dweeb brain. I meant do I look okay for you."

"Oh, I knew that."

She shook her head.

She sat on her knees behind him as he said a prayer in front of Nancy's headstone. She put her hands on his shoulders and listened.

"Does it seem weird that I talk to her like she's here and can actually hear me?"

"Yes, but it's okay," she teased. "I'm sure there's a shrink who could help you."

"You're a brat." He pulled her in front of him and they sat Indian-style facing the marker. "You can join in the conversation if you want. We can kinda talk to each other."

"What about?"

"I kinda ramble about what's going on in my life and people she knew. I always tell her how bad you are."

"I've been a good girl, Tuck," she whispered leaning back into him."

"I know."

"Have you told her we set a date for the wedding?" Caralyn asked.

"Not yet, but I will."

They talked to each other as if Nancy could hear for fifteen minutes. They stood up and hugged each other with eyes closed. Neither one wanted to let go.

After a brief eternity passed, Tucker opened his eyes. She opened her eyes a moment later.

"Did you hear that?"

"I did. What kind of train did it sound like today, Tucker?"

He let go, looked at the sky and listened to the birds singing. "It sounded like an old freight train to me."

She smacked his arm.

Chapter Twenty-Five

"Tucker, how are you going to keep from seeing Caralyn today?" Derren asked. "She's right next door and we're in her house."

Tucker sat at the kitchen table and cut his pancakes in half. He added enough syrup to float the pancakes out to sea. "What did you say?"

Derren shook his head. "Man, you are in another galaxy. When are you due to return to earth?"

"Sorry, but my mind is going in a dozen directions without any GPS guidance."

"I asked how you intend to avoid seeing the delinquent until it's time."

He took a bite of pancakes and the syrup dripped down his chin. "I didn't think of it. Should we not see each other before the ceremony?"

"I don't suppose it matters. Have you heard from Richard? He is coming, right?"

"He should be here by ten."

Derren sat across the table and looked out the window. "It's hard to believe it's been over a year. I can picture Nancy on the day you guys got married."

"So can I. We weren't together for a full year," Tucker said. He toyed with his pancakes and asked, "Do you think we're doing the right thing?"

"Absolutely!" Derren answered without hesitation. "You told me months ago it was what Nancy wanted. Don't tell me you're having doubts. You've always loved Caralyn."

Tucker sighed, thought about one of his earliest memories and grinned. "I can vaguely remember playing with a nerf ball shortly after the funeral. She was a baby, and I was trying to impress her."

"I've heard the story from your father," Derren said.

"She woke up and I sat next to Mom and tried to make her laugh."

"Did she?"

"Yeah, she made faces like she had gas and was pooping, but then she grinned and made noises like she was happy."

"I'm always happy after... never mind."

"We used to play in the sandbox. She tried to eat the sand."

"What time are we supposed to meet at the church?" Derren asked.

"One o'clock," Tucker said then laughed. "Do you think she will dress up, or wear shorts and a t-shirt?"

"I'd say the odds are fifty-fifty, but your mom will make her dress up."

They sat quietly for a moment lost in thoughts.

"I hate to pry, but how are things with Natalie?"

"No better. She refuses to meet with the marriage counselor." Derren got up and poured another cup of coffee. "Have you talked to Mr. or Mrs. Young since they moved to Missouri?"

"No, but I sent a card. They're probably busy taking care of Sandy's little boy. She's expecting again."

"What do you want to do to kill time? You should have gotten married in the morning."

"We thought about it, but she wanted it to be in the afternoon."

"Where are you staying tonight?"

Tucker smiled and hooked a thumb over his shoulder. "In her new bedroom."

"For real? I heard Mom talking to Aunt Sarah about the house. You bought it, right?"

"If you want to call it that. Beth signed away her share. Cara already owned half. She always said she didn't want to sell it because I might need it someday."

"I don't think she imagined it would turn out like this, huh?"

Tucker shrugged. "Nobody did."

"Can I ask something that's really none of my business?"

"I can guess. You want to know if we've... you know, right?"

181

"I know you have in the past."

Tucker smiled and closed his eyes. "I can picture the way the room looked and how it smelled."

"I hope you're referring to the candles and not our dirty laundry," Derren joked.

"Yeah, I stuffed all the dirty clothes in the closet."

"You thought Richard and I didn't know."

"We didn't want anyone to know. It was complicated. There was our family to consider. She was so young."

"She's always been older than her years," Derren said. "Mentally, I mean. She still looks like a college kid."

"She should still be in college."

"That night was a long time ago," Derren said and then drained his coffee.

"Tonight will be like starting over. Don't tell anyone, but I'm kinda nervous about it. The first time was funny because of how I bumped her head on the doorframe and then we couldn't... figure it out at first."

"Typical of virgins."

"We aren't virgins now, but in a strange way, I feel we are."

"Why haven't you been practicing?"

"I didn't think it was right since I started going to church."

"Yeah, you are different since you found religion."

"Mom, do I have to wear a dress?" Caralyn asked as she held up the 'one.' "What if Tucker recognizes it and gets mad?"

"Have you worn it since... that night?" Mom asked.

"The only other time I wore it was on my eighteenth birthday when the guys took me to dinner."

Mom took the dress and inspected it. "It looks brand new."

"I've only worn it a few hours. It fits perfectly," Caralyn said as she sat on the edge of the bed in her pajamas. She closed her eyes and sighed.

"What is it, sweetie?" Mom sat next to her and put an arm around her shoulders. "I can tell there's something on your mind other than getting married."

"Sometimes I wonder what would have happened if I hadn't made him leave that night. If I had gone after him a few seconds earlier and not let him get in the elevator. If I had been smarter and faster, I would have let him spend the night. We would have fallen back in love, and I never would have thought about Justin again."

Mom grinned. "Jeremiah, dear."

Caralyn laughed and plopped onto her back. "I wish I had listened to Daddy. He should have locked me in my room until I came to my senses."

"You were much wiser at eighteen," Mom said.

"I was insufferable at times, huh?"

"It happens to everyone."

She sat up and chewed on her lip.

"I know that look. What else is troubling you?"

"Do you think we should have been sleeping together since we got engaged? What if it... doesn't work out like it's supposed to. Physically, I mean."

"I don't think you will have any issues."

"I haven't had sex since I broke up with Trent. That was in 2009. Wow! I haven't had sex in over two and a half years."

"Cara, you are only twenty-two. Some girls are still virgins at that age." Mom laughed and added, "Probably not too many in this age, but they do exist."

"I almost feel like a virgin. If I'm honest, I'm scared to death."

"Why? You love each other."

She plopped back onto the bed and crossed her arms over her breasts. "It's not that. I love him, and he loves me."

"Have you been thinking about Nancy?"

"More lately than in the last year."

"You told me what she asked of you."

"I remember every word she said. How could she be so selfless or however you put it?"

"I think it was because of her faith in God. Her family was always more into church than we were."

"We went to church when Tuck and I were kids, but then we stopped. We got busy with life and didn't have time for God."

"That's changed for Tucker," Mom said. "Has it changed for you as well?"

"Yes, but maybe not to the same degree. I believe in God and all, but I don't read the Bible like Tuck does. He doesn't go around hitting people over the head with his beliefs, but he kinda lets his life speak for itself. Am I making any sense?"

"Definitely, sweetie." Mom stood up. "I am going to make breakfast. What would you like?"

"I don't know if I can eat. My stomach's full of butterflies flying around bumping into each other."

"You need something besides butterflies in your stomach. I'll make a couple slices of toast to start."

"I heard a car pull into the driveway. Could it be Richard?" Derren asked.

Tucker checked the time. "He must have left Chicago earlier than he planned."

Derren opened the back door and stepped onto the porch. He waved when Richard appeared around the corner. "You're early."

"I didn't want to take a chance and be late. How are you?" Richard bounded up the steps and hugged Derren. "How's the groom?"

Derren laughed and answered, "He claims to be nervous about tonight. Maybe you should talk to him."

"Nervous? Why? Not about sex is it?"

Derren laughed. "You better talk to him."

Derren opened the door and they walked into the kitchen.

Tucker stood up and held out a hand.

Richard shook it but then gave Tucker a bear hug. "It's good to see you. It's been too long."

"Funny how life interferes."

"Tell me about it. I could use a cup of coffee after I drain the tank."

Tucker pointed. "You know where it is. You've stayed here enough times."

Richard returned a moment later and took a seat.

Derren handed him a cup of coffee. "There's breakfast if you're hungry."

"Maybe later. Thanks." He took a sip while peering at Tucker. "You ready for this?"

Tucker took a deep breath. "Do you mean the ceremony or tonight?"

"Tonight, I guess. You can't be nervous about the ceremony. This is the right thing to do. I won't say it's what Nancy wanted..." He set the coffee down. "Actually, I will say it. Cara told me what Nancy said. You are meant to be together. I'm not particularly religious like you've become, but I was raised Catholic. I know some stuff, and I think God works in strange ways at times. We may never understand why she was taken so early, but she was. Nothing we can do about it. Life goes on. Deal with it."

Tucker smiled and said, "I'm so glad you're here."

"Me, too. How's the delinquent? What's she been doing the last year. Man! Has it really been a year since I was in Stockton Woods?"

"A bit over a year," Derren answered.

"Does she still live in Chicago? I should know, but I've been working my normal eighty hours." He picked up his coffee and took a long drink. "The firm wiped out my college debt. I have to work eight hundred hours a week for the next thirty years, but I am debt free." He looked around the kitchen. "It looks different than what I remember."

"I moved in August. Too many memories to stay," Tucker said. "She moved out of her apartment in September. She didn't want to stay by herself, so she moved back home. She added an addition to the house and did some work on the older part. I'll let you see." Tucker laughed. "Someone should write a book about our situation. There can't be too many people like us. We grew up switching back and forth between houses."

185

"She could write it, but who would believe it? It's stranger than fiction," Richard said. "Show me the house. Can I crash here tonight?"

Derren laughed and said, "You might not be welcome."

Richard looked at him then Tucker and tilted his head. "Why?"

"They're spending the night here," Derren said.

"No way! For real?"

Tucker nodded.

"That is stranger than science fiction."

"Cara, can you answer the phone, please?" Mom asked. "I'm talking to your father."

"I got it," she hollered. "Hello, McKay residence."

"Sarah?"

"Sorry, this is Caralyn. Did you want to talk to Mom?" Caralyn looked at the phone. *If I didn't know better, I would think it's Mr. Green.*

"Actually, I can talk to you. This is Tom Green..."

"Mr. Green!" Caralyn squealed. "Is it really you?"

"In the flesh. Or on the phone, I suppose. How are you?"

"Great! You won't believe what's happened?"

"Can I guess?"

"You can try, but you'll never get it right."

"I'm sorry, Caralyn, but I talked to your father about a month ago. He told me. Was it last week?"

Caralyn shook her head and giggled. "No! It's today at one," she said. "Just immediate family. No reception for now. We might have one later."

"Shoot! I'm interrupting your big day. I'm sorry. I should let you go..."

"Please don't hang up. I haven't talked to you since you moved to Fremont. Are you still living there?"

"No, I moved to Colorado after a year in Fremont."

"I didn't know. I should have stayed in contact. I had your email, but I might have lost it."

186

"I'll give it to you again, and when you have time, send me a message."

"I will. Would you like to talk to Dad or Mom?"

"Not today. I'll call another time when you aren't busy."

"It was good to hear your voice, Mr. Green."

He chuckled and answered, "Yours, too. I'm still Mr. Green, huh?"

"Always."

Richard walked into the living room and gazed at the walls. "Different paint. I like it. It's neutral, but with a touch of ... " He shrugged and added, "No clue. I can tell it's been painted."

"She bought new furniture and painted the whole house," Tucker said as he sat on the brown leather couch. He pointed to the picture window. "She bought new blinds." He looked around the room. "New stuff on the walls. I can't remember everything she's done."

"She had the wiring and plumbing updated," Derren said. "The whole house has been updated. It's bigger now, but still cozy."

Richard leaned back in the matching recliner, popped up the foot rest and got comfortable. "Why are we here and she's at your parents' house? She lives here all the time, right?"

"Normally, she would be here. I came home a few times during the season, and stayed with Mom and Dad. She was settled into the house. Grandma's house. There were times she had to stay with Mom and Dad because of the remodeling and stuff, but otherwise, she lived here."

"Why the change for this weekend?" Richard asked with a shrug. "I don't get it."

Derren shrugged. Tucker stared at the ceiling.

"Am I missing something obvious? I am an attorney. I should be able to spot stuff and think analytically."

"Today's the ninth," Derren said. "Tuck and Nancy got married on July 11 two years ago. I think Cara was spooked."

"Why not change the date?"

"Today's Barbara Dawson's birthday. Would have been. You know what I mean," Tucker replied.

"Her birth mother, right?" Richard asked.

Tucker nodded.

"Sorry, but sometimes I forget she never knew her birth parents."

"Cara told me she wanted to spend one night away from our house so she could feel like she was... I don't know how to explain it," Tucker said. "A couple months ago we watched *Father of the Bride* and she loves those movies. The original ones with Elizabeth Taylor and the new ones. There's a scene in one of them where the bride talks about leaving her childhood home. I think Carrie thinks of next door as her childhood home."

"I get it now," Richard said.

"Really?" Derren asked.

Richard laughed and shook his head. "Not one iota."

"Who was on the phone, sweetie?" Mom asked as she and Mr. McKay walked into the kitchen. "Chairs are to sit on."

Caralyn grinned, got off the table and said, "Mr. Green. He thought I was you at first."

Dad sat across from Caralyn. "I talked to him about a month ago. He was inquiring about a position at Dickinson College."

"How is he doing?" Mom asked while pulling out the carton of eggs from the fridge. "Your father is hungry. Can you eat now?"

"One egg and a piece of toast. Dry. No butter. I have to watch my figure," she said with a giggle.

Dad smiled at her. "I doubt if one egg and dry toast is enough to fill you up."

"She's nervous about... tonight," Mom said without turning from the stove.

"Why would you be nervous about tonight? You aren't going anywhere," Dad said while checking the salt and pepper shakers.

"Daddy!"

"What?" he asked with a shrug.

"She's nervous about her wedding night," Mom replied after cracking the eggs. "She and Tuck will have sex."

"Mom!" Caralyn covered her face with her hands. "Can you talk about something else, please?"

"Sweetie, it's okay for married people to sleep together. That's how babies are made."

"Mom!"

"That's where you came from," Dad said then caught himself. "Well, not because your mother and I had sex, but..."

"Mom! Make him stop."

"Jim, I think you're embarrassing her, and she's nervous enough as it is."

He tilted his head. "I don't understand. You did tell me about Trent, sweetie. I may think of you as my innocent little girl, but I know you're a woman."

Caralyn sighed and buried her face in her hands.

Mom walked behind her and rubbed her back. She looked at her husband, took a deep breath and said, "You may be a college professor, dear, but you have no clue when it comes to the intricacies of being a young lady in love."

"Duh! I've never been one." He looked at the stove. "I think the eggs are done."

Chapter Twenty-Six

"Jim, you should check on the guys," Mom said.

"Why? I'm sure they can get showered and dressed without my help."

"We have things to do and you are in the way. Cara needs to shower before Mrs. Boyd arrives to fix her hair." Mom waved a hand. "Please, go away and let us women be."

He closed his book, rose from his recliner and asked, "Should I take my clothes with me?"

Mom walked into the living room. "I thought you were already dressed for the ceremony."

"I am except for my jacket. I didn't want to put it on until we got to the church. What time is it?"

"Almost eleven. We have to be there at one sharp."

"Why? It's just us, the kids and the guys. It's not like that new preacher can start without us. I made a joke."

Mom did an about-face. "Men. You can be so clueless."

"Fine. I will hang out next door until you women are ready to leave. I'm surprised the guys aren't playing basketball or something."

Mom hollered from the kitchen, "They would be, but I warned Tucker he would suffer greatly if he got hurt." She walked back into the living room. "They did play ball when he and Nancy got married, didn't they?"

"Yes, and so did Caralyn."

"What did I do?" Caralyn asked as she walked into the room.

"You played ball with the guys when Tucker and Nancy got married," Mom answered. "Why are you still in your pajamas? Get showered. Mrs. Boyd will be here soon."

"Can I play ball with the guys first? Why aren't they shooting baskets or something?" She moved so she could see through the house to the backyard court.

"You are not shooting baskets with the guys, Caralyn Ann Dawson! I forbid it."

"Your mother warned them they would face dire consequences if they touched a ball of any size or shape this morning," Dad said.

"They're probably bored to death. Should I check on them?" she asked.

"Caralyn Ann! You are not going over there in your pajamas," Mom insisted. "And march yourself into the bathroom this instant. Take a shower and put something on so you can get your hair done."

"I will make sure he's ready on time, Mr. McKay."

"Thanks, Richard. I would go back to the house, but I've been ordered to stay away until Caralyn gets dressed."

"How much longer before we have to head to the church?" Richard asked.

"It's almost noon," Tucker answered. "Another hour to go."

"We could watch TV or grab something to eat," Derren suggested.

"Let's eat," Tucker said. "I could go for a burger."

"Are we going out for dinner tonight? What's the plan?" Richard asked. "You aren't having a reception."

Tucker turned off the TV. "Caralyn wants to go to that new Italian place in Glenns Hill. Is The Curve okay for lunch?"

"Sounds like a plan," Richard said.

"I'll go with," Dad said.

"Do you want something to eat before we head to the church?" Mom asked.

"I'm not real hungry, but I should have something in my stomach," Caralyn replied As Mrs. Boyd worked on her hair.

"I made turkey sandwiches for your father and me. Would you like one?"

"Okay, but don't add any cheese."

"Sit still, young lady," Mrs. Boyd ordered. "You are just as fidgety as when you were a child."

191

"I'm ready to leave," Tucker said. "Are you driving, Derren?"

"I can drive. How is Cara getting there?"

"She's riding with Mom and Dad," Tucker answered.

"Is anyone else going to be there?" Richard asked. "I got the feeling the ceremony has been kept a secret from people."

Tucker shook his head. "Grandma and Grandpa know about it, but we haven't told too many other people. Beth and Ray know, but they're in California."

"What are they doing there?" Richard asked.

"He's working on a fashion shoot for some magazine, and Beth is coordinating the models or something."

"We should get going," Dad said after checking the time. "I saw the guys leave a few minutes ago."

Caralyn walked out of the bedroom and faced her parents. "How do I look?"

"You look radiant. Your eyes are shining," Mom said. "What do you think, Jim?"

He nodded and clenched his jaw.

"Let's go," Caralyn said.

They arrived at the church three minutes later. Dad parked along the street. He opened the rear door for Caralyn and led the way up the concrete stairs to the east door of the church. He opened the heavy wooden door for Sarah and Caralyn.

"Thanks, Dad," she said with a smile.

"Where are we supposed to go?" he asked.

"I thought we should use the classroom right here." She smiled and said, "I can hear the guys talking about basketball."

Mom and Dad entered first. The guys turned, stopped jabbering and froze when Caralyn walked into the room.

"What? Do I have dirt on my face?" she asked walking up to Derren and Richard. "Why are you staring at me?"

"You look pretty good for a delinquent," Richard teased.

She made a face then turned to Tucker. "I'm ready if you are."

"I'm ready, Carrie." He looked toward the preacher and nodded.

Rob Lucas smiled and faced everyone. "Should I go through the 'who gives this woman' routine?"

"Daddy does," Caralyn said.

Pastor Lucas smiled again. "If you want to take your places, I will start."

"Where are we supposed to stand, sweetie?" Dad asked. "We didn't have a rehearsal."

"You and Mom can stand next to me, and Derren and Richard can stand by Tuck," she replied.

"Switch places with me," Richard said to Derren. "You're family. I'm just a friend."

Caralyn grinned and said, "You are my bridesmaid, Rickey."

"Should I have worn a dress?"

"I guess that makes me the best man," Derren said.

"You guys are dweebs," Caralyn said.

"Now that we're all in place, let me pray..."

The guys shuffled their feet during the prayer.

Pastor Lucas smiled at Caralyn and said, "Caralyn Ann Dawson, do you take this man to be your lawful wedded husband? To have and hold from this day forward until death do you part?"

"I do."

"Tucker James McKay," as Pastor Lucas said his name, Caralyn got goosebumps up and down her arms, a chill ran up her back and her heart fluttered... "do you take this woman to be your lawful wedded wife? To have and to hold from this day forward till death do you part?"

"I do," Tucker said with a smile as Caralyn chewed her lip.

The rings were presented, placed on fingers, the vows were spoken and Pastor Lucas said, "By the power vested in me by the crazy state of Illinois and by God Almighty, I pronounce you man and wife. You may now..."

For a second everyone watched as the bride and groom kissed.

Then Richard looked around the room. Derren pulled out his phone and checked the weather. Dad scratched his jaw and smiled at the preacher. Mom placed a hand to her mouth, sighed and watched the kiss.

"Hey! When he said kiss, I don't think he meant for the rest of the day," Richard said.

Caralyn faced Richard and stuck out her tongue. "Make sure you're out of the house before we get back from dinner, bucko."

Mom and Dad hugged the newlyweds while Derren and Richard stood back and watched.

"Contacts bothering you again?" Richard asked.

Derren nodded.

"Yeah, mine, too," Richard said as he wiped his glasses with his handkerchief.

Caralyn shook hands with Pastor Lucas and turned toward the guys. She shook her head and said, "I expected Mom and Dad to shed a few tears, but guys aren't supposed to show any emotion."

"Contacts," Richard said.

"Allergies," Derren replied.

"Whatever," she said then hugged them.

"Where are we going now?" Dad asked.

"To see Grandma and Grandpa," Caralyn answered. "We promised to stop by."

"My brothers are meeting us there," Mom said. "Davey and Melissa will be there with the baby. We should take our car and Derren will drive Cara and Tuck." She asked Richard, "Would you like to ride with us or with Derren?"

Richard grinned and answered, "Oh, I want to ride with them. I want to see if they behave on the way out there."

"We're going to behave, Richard. I've waited all this time. I can wait another few hours."

"Yeah, I find that difficult to believe."

"We will meet you at the farm," Dad said.

Derren parked his minivan on the side of the road by the front gate. Caralyn jumped out and opened the freshly painted gate. She raced up the sidewalk and waved at Grandma and Grandpa sitting in their metal rocking chairs on the front porch.

"Hi, Grandma! Hi, Grandpa!" Caralyn shouted in much the same manner she had done as a child. "We came to see you. How are you feeling?"

Grandpa stood up and opened his arms as Caralyn vaulted up the three steps and onto the porch. She nearly knocked him over with a hug.

"What brings you here, Cara?" he asked though he knew the answer.

She proudly held out her hand to show them the simple wedding band. "Tucker and I got married today."

"You did, huh?"

"You know we did." She lifted her foot. "He bought me new pink sneakers. Do you like them? I love them even if they don't match my dress."

Tucker joined them on the porch, kissed Grandma's cheek and put his hands on Caralyn's shoulders. "Is she being a pest?"

Caralyn looked up at Tucker and whispered, "I'm not a pest, am I, Grandpa?"

Grandpa responded by kissing the top of her head as he wiped away a tear.

Grandma sat in her rocker, waved a finger and said, "Just because you kids are married now doesn't mean you can go skinny dipping in the pond like you used to."

"Grandma! You knew?" Caralyn bit her lip.

Grandma's eyes twinkled. "I've always known. Your parents did the same thing and thought they got away with it, too."

The front door opened and Davey walked out holding his daughter. "That didn't take long." He looked at his brother. "Did you shed a few tears? I did thinking about how poor Tucker has to put up with her."

Caralyn poked Davey's arm. "Let me have Lyndsey before you drop her. You're coming to the restaurant, right?"

"If you insist."

Uncle Carlton stood in the doorway, grinned and said, "Who's this pretty little lady, and why are you dressed up so fancy on a Saturday afternoon? You better not try to steal my granddaughter."

"Can I borrow her for a while?" Caralyn asked.

"I suppose," he answered stepping onto the porch. "Come on inside. Mary made some of them fancy *horse devours* and Grandma made cookies. You better grab some before the guys eat everything."

Tucker patted Grandpa's back. "Have you been following what the doctor said?"

Grandpa Clyde Stanfield waved dismissively. "What does that whippersnapper know about living on a farm? He must think everything gets done using magic."

Mom and Dad McKay arrived before everyone headed inside.

Grandma Anna Stanfield waited for her daughter to walk up the sidewalk. "I know you said not to, but I made some cookies and Mary made something to snack on."

Sarah hugged her mother and whispered, "I knew you would. It's all right. Is everyone here? Alton wasn't sure they would get back from Tennessee in time."

"I don't think they're coming. Alton said Violetta was under the weather."

"Too bad. I hope she feels better soon." Sarah hugged her father. "How are you feeling, Dad?"

"Best day I've had in months," he replied.

"Are you going to carry her over the threshold?" Richard asked.

"Am I supposed to do that here?" Tucker asked Caralyn.

She faced him and answered, "You can if you want, but you definitely have to when we get home."

"Don't do it, Tucker. You might hurt your back," Richard teased.

"I don't weigh that much," Caralyn said.

196

Tucker scratched his ear. "I don't know. The first time I carried you through a doorway, I bumped your head against it."

Caralyn turned red as she faced Mom and Grandma. "I don't know what he's talking about."

Dad McKay looked at the guys, who suddenly developed an interest in the old chicken house.

"Where are the plates? I want some of the fancy food," Uncle Carlton said.

"Let's go inside," Grandma said.

"I'll carry you later, Cara."

After spending two hours at the farm, everyone returned to town.

"Can we change clothes now?" Tucker asked. "Do I have to wear my suit to dinner?"

"Do you want me to wear my dress?" Caralyn asked.

Tucker nodded.

"Then you have to wear your suit. Derren and Richard can change, but you're the groom. You have to look like one."

"Good. I'm changing," Richard said. "Should I call about a hotel room now, or take a chance I can find one in Butler after dinner?"

"You could stay in Tucker's room," Mom said. "He won't need it tonight."

"Or any other night from now on," Dad said with a grin.

"Thanks for the offer, but I'll stay in a hotel. I don't want to be this close to Grandma Florence's house tonight."

Caralyn slugged Richard's side. "What did you mean?"

He shrugged. "Nothing, but I would sleep better in a hotel than in Tucker's room."

"I'm going to head home," Derren said.

"Aren't you going to dinner with us?" Caralyn asked. "Who will drive us? We can't drive ourselves because we have to sit in the back and make out."

Richard laughed and said, "Something tells me you better stay for dinner, Derren."

"Okay, I'll stay, but you have to behave."

"Party pooper."

Derren laughed and offered, "It doesn't make sense for us to take two vehicles. I will drive and bring everyone home."

"Thanks, Derren. I should have kept my minivan instead of buying another car," Mr. McKay said.

They arrived at Luigi's Italian Bistro in Glenns Hill by six and were seated in a private room. Davey and Melissa arrived ten minutes later.

"Where is Lyndsey?" Caralyn asked.

"Mom and Dad volunteered to babysit so Melissa and I could have time to ourselves," Davey answered.

"Daddy, is it okay if I have wine with my dinner?" Caralyn asked with a grin.

Dad frowned and answered, "Not a chance, young lady. You have to be twenty-one to drink alcohol in this state."

"But, Daddy! I'm twenty-two and married."

"You can't be. You're just a child," he said and then grinned.

"What kind of wine do you suggest?" Mom asked. "I might try a glass. I haven't had any wine since college."

"Really?" Caralyn asked.

Mom grinned. "Are you asking if I want a glass of wine now, or that I drank wine in college?"

"Both."

"We did drink wine occasionally, but gave it up before Tucker was born. We haven't had any alcohol in the house since then."

"I usually kept a bottle in my apartment, but I haven't bought any since I moved home. I would have to drink it all myself. Nobody else drinks."

"I would help," Richard offered. "We need a bottle so I can make a toast to the bride and groom."

"I should do it because I'm the best man," Derren said.

198

It was shortly after eight thirty when Derren pulled into the McKay's driveway.

"Thanks for driving, Derren," Caralyn said as she stood outside the driver's door. "Be careful going home."

"I will, and let me know what time you guys are getting back. I'll save Uncle Jim a trip to the airport."

"Thanks for the offer, but we're going to drive," Caralyn said as she waved and watched Derren back out of the driveway.

"Give me one minute to get everything out of the house, and it's all yours," Richard said.

Tucker smiled and said, "Better make it thirty seconds or less. Someone is getting impatient."

Caralyn smacked his arm. "I've waited this long. I can wait five more minutes."

Richard dashed into the house.

"Sarah, I think we should head inside," Jim said. "It looks like it might storm later."

Caralyn hugged her mother then held up her arms for her father. "Thanks for everything," she whispered.

"Let me know if you want breakfast," Mom said.

"Thanks, Mom, but we can manage," Tucker said.

They heard the back door open and saw Richard carry his suitcase and his garment bag to his car. He tossed them in the trunk and walked across the yard.

"Thanks for making the trip," Tucker said.

Richard patted Tucker's back. "I wouldn't have missed it for a murder case."

Caralyn laughed. "You'll never see the inside of a courtroom. You're into corporate law."

He walked up to Caralyn, hugged her and whispered, "I guess I missed my chance for good, huh?"

"Yes, and you better never tell anyone how many times we tried."

"I will carry our secret to the grave." He let her go and waved goodbye.

"Are we going to live here forever, Tuck?" Caralyn asked as they cuddled in her new bedroom. She took in the aroma of blueberry candles. "I'm so glad we never sold Grandma's house."

"I think this will be the perfect place for you to write all your novels." He tugged at her pajama bottom.

She lifted up. "It's a pretty small town, and everyone knows everything about us."

He tossed her pajamas over his shoulder toward the closet. "I don't mind. I won't be playing for the Bulls forever. I think I'll have had enough of living in the big city by the time I retire."

"What will you do here?" She giggled at the sight of his Bart Simpson boxers. "There aren't many jobs available."

"Dad told me the head basketball coach at Dickinson College might have an opening on his staff."

"What do you know about coaching basketball?" she teased. "You've never been that good of a player."

"I've got a few years to learn something about the game, you brat," he said. "It will be good to have Mom and Dad living next door if we ever need a babysitter."

"Are we going to work on making them grandparents right away, Tuck?" Caralyn asked.

Tucker grinned. "I think we should, Carrie."

"Are you going to do it right this time?" she put a finger to her mouth. "It's been a few years..."

"I got this," he whispered.

Epilogue

The sun shone brightly through the kitchen windows as Tucker put his arms around Caralyn's waist from behind and nuzzled her neck.

"Stop it! I just took a shower. You have to wait."

"I want to go to the cemetery this morning," he replied.

She turned to face him. "Do you want me to go with?"

"Yes. We can eat breakfast first."

They rode their new mountain bikes to the cemetery to place fresh flowers by the headstones of Douglas and Barbara Dawson, Grandma Florence Jackson and Nancy Young McKay.

"I won!" Caralyn shouted as she slid to a stop on the gravel road. She jumped off her bike and laid it gently in the grass.

"Only because I let you," Tucker replied.

He held her hand as they walked directly to the gravesite. *You're not afraid anymore, are you?*

"I see a cardinal on Grandma's stone," Caralyn said.

Tucker turned to look, but the bird had flown away.

"It was there," she said. "It might come back."

He waited a few seconds as he thought he heard the whistle of a long gone train. He smiled and whispered, "It sounds like a cheerful train today."

Check out these other titles by the author. Visit the website:
kennethleemcgee.com

The Emmy's Story Series

1. We Were 'posed to Get Married
2. One Of The Guys
3. A New Friend
4. Did You Like the Ravioli Tonight?
5. Completely and Forever: A Wedding
6. It's Time To Go!
7. How Difficult Can It Be?
8. Forever... Isabella... Forever
9. The Forgettable Year
10. Turning Thirty
11. Hello, I'm James
12. Remember The Struggle
13. But God! I Write Songs
14. A Lifelong Dream
15. Gideon's Tree
16. New Priorities
17. Christmas Surprise
18. God Is In Control
19. Life Goes On

The Annie Mercer O'Dell Series

1. Roosevelt High
2. North Park College
3. Smoky Mountain Summer

The Stockton Woods Series

1. Sounds Like a Mournful Train Today
2. Sounds Like a Happy Train Today

The Rex Ford & Clay Horn Books

1. The Amazing Adventures Of Rex Ford & Clay Horn

Stand Alone Books

1. Growing Up In Kinmundy Junction
2. Grandpa, Lions and Kitty Cats: A Collection Of Short Stories For Children Of All Ages
3. The True Stories Of Ol' Melvin, Obadiah, Perkins MacGhee and other Characters